"Let's try to be

"I'm trying," Marcus told her in his low, gruff voice. "You have to give a guy a few days to figure things out and get over feeling like he's had his legs kicked out from under him."

"I know." She pulled her seat belt around and he reached over to click it into place for her. "Thank you."

"I'm not going to take him from you," he said as they headed down the long driveway back to the main road.

The sting of tears took her by surprise. She wiped at them and when he handed her a handkerchief, she shook her head.

"I'm fine."

"Yeah, of course you are." He shoved the handkerchief into her hand. "I know he needs you. I know he doesn't need a scarred-up, dysfunctional cowboy for a dad."

"I think you're wrong," she told him.

And the words took her by surprise.

She hadn't expected to like Marcus Palermo...

Brenda Minton lives in the Ozarks with her husband, children, cats, dogs and strays. She is a pastor's wife, Sunday-school teacher, coffee addict and sleep deprived. Not in that order. Her dream to be an author for Harlequin started somewhere in the pages of a romance novel about a young American woman stranded in a Spanish castle. Her dreams came true, and twenty-plus books later, she is an author hoping to inspire young girls to dream.

Visit the Author Profile page at Harlequin.com for more titles.

The Rancher's Secret Child

Brenda Minton

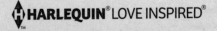

If you purchased this book without a cover you should be aware that this book is stolen property. It was reported as "unsold and destroyed" to the publisher, and neither the author nor the publisher has received any payment for this "stripped book."

Recycling programs
for this product may
not exist in your area.

 LOVE INSPIRED BOOKS

ISBN-13: 978-1-335-42806-6

The Rancher's Secret Child

Copyright © 2018 by Brenda Minton

All rights reserved. Except for use in any review, the reproduction or utilization of this work in whole or in part in any form by any electronic, mechanical or other means, now known or hereafter invented, including xerography, photocopying and recording, or in any information storage or retrieval system, is forbidden without the written permission of the editorial office, Love Inspired Books, 195 Broadway, New York, NY 10007 U.S.A.

This is a work of fiction. Names, characters, places and incidents are either the product of the author's imagination or are used fictitiously, and any resemblance to actual persons, living or dead, business establishments, events or locales is entirely coincidental.

This edition published by arrangement with Love Inspired Books.

® and TM are trademarks of Love Inspired Books, used under license. Trademarks indicated with ® are registered in the United States Patent and Trademark Office, the Canadian Intellectual Property Office and in other countries.

www.Harlequin.com

Printed in U.S.A.

It is of the Lord's mercies that we are not
consumed, because his compassions fail not.
They are new every morning:
great is thy faithfulness.
　　　　　　　—*Lamentations* 3:22–23

This book is dedicated to my Aunt Joyce, Aunt Alice and Aunt Betty. And in memory of my Aunt Shirley Clark. They have taught us to have fun, to be classy when it matters, to live life to the fullest and to love family.

Chapter One

A car door slammed and a child's laughter rang out, followed by a woman's voice. The horse beneath Marcus Palermo skittered across the arena, forcing him to hold tight. He managed a quick look in the direction of the visitors. A woman, tall with dark hair. A little boy with chocolate-brown hair who seemed all excited as he headed for the arena as Marcus made a last-ditch attempt at controlling the horse.

He had a few seconds to wonder where this woman and boy had come from and how they'd found the place, an old farm situated down a long dirt drive and hidden from view of the road by a copse of trees. He'd only recently purchased the old Brown farm and few people knew he lived here.

The boy shouted something as he ran toward

the makeshift arena that Marcus had built with cattle panels. The horse jerked his head forward and took a few running bucks across the dirt-packed pen. Marcus's hat flew off. He'd just bought that hat and he liked it. He tightened his legs, but the horse had the upper hand. The black-and-white paint gelding twisted and, with a final hard buck, sent Marcus flying. As he hit the ground, he remembered that he really didn't like ranching all that much.

After a minute he sat up, rubbing the back of his neck where it hurt the most. Slowly he became aware of a couple of things. First, the horse he'd been attempting to ride had moseyed on over to the fence. The traitor had his head down like a big old puppy dog so the kid could pet him. The woman's gaze left the boy and the horse and shifted his way, nervous and a bit guilty.

Considering she was partially to blame for his bad exit off the horse's back, she could have at least asked if he was okay. But, no, she only managed to look sheepish as she ran her hand down the horse's neck. The little boy seemed more curious than anything.

"No, don't worry, I'm fine," he muttered as he came to his feet.

He limped across the arena and grabbed the horse's reins because he was a little jealous of the attention the animal was getting. He moved the gelding away from the fence and away from the hands of the visitors. The woman moved her sunglasses to the top of her head and narrowed her blue eyes at him. He must be getting better at offending the fairer sex. It had taken only two minutes for him to earn her displeasure. "Did he break your leg?" the little boy asked.

Marcus glanced at the kid. He was maybe five, with big eyes. Those eyes widened a bit, the normal reaction to Marcus's face. Because it was a kid, not an adult staring at him, Marcus had sympathy. He half turned, giving the little boy his good side.

"No," he answered roughly. "It would take more than that to break me."

"I bet it would," the boy said in awe.

Marcus hoped the woman and kid weren't fans with the misplaced idea that he welcomed uninvited guests to the ranch for sightseeing. But the woman didn't appear to be an admiring fan. She didn't look like the type of woman who had ever witnessed a professional bull ride, let alone knew who the champions might be.

"Is there something I can help you with?" He looked down at the little boy and back at the woman, because there was something familiar about her.

She was taller than average, with long, dark hair, and had high cheekbones that made him think she had Native American ancestry. But she had startling blue eyes. The blue of a winter sky. Those eyes were boring into him like he was a bug and she couldn't figure out what kind. So obviously *not* a fan.

Fine with him. He didn't need fans. In fact, he didn't need much of anything or anyone. Which was exactly why he'd picked this property, several miles off the beaten path and far enough away from his siblings that they wouldn't always be in his business.

"Are you Marcus Palermo?" she asked, her hand protective on the boy's shoulder.

"That would be me."

"Then we need to talk." She squatted to look the boy in the eye. "Sit and don't move."

"By myself?" For the first time, the little guy looked unsure. And Marcus had to admit to getting his hackles up when a kid looked unhappy.

"By himself?" he echoed. The question earned him an answering look from the female. She straightened and met his gaze head-on, those blue eyes once again penetrating him. He didn't like feeling as if he was five and about to get in trouble.

He also didn't like the fact that his gaze landed on cherry-glossed lips that were far from smiling, yet were still cherry. As if that bright gloss was the only frivolous thing she allowed herself.

"He'll be fine," she answered. "We're going to head to the barn and talk for a few minutes. I'll be able to see him from there. Correct?"

"Sure thing," Marcus whispered.

"Do you ever talk loud?" the boy asked, looking up at him from the spot where she'd told him to sit. He had a small car, and as he stared at Marcus, he pushed the car through the dirt.

"No, I don't." Marcus walked off, leading the horse behind him. He heard the gate creak on its hinges and the footsteps hurrying to catch up.

He entered the side door to the barn and she followed him.

"Say what it is you came here to say." He ground the words out. He didn't mean to sound gruff, but it couldn't be helped. Added to that, something about this woman put him off-kilter. And not in a totally bad way.

He gave her another long look and saw the wary shift of her gaze from his face to the door. She had bad news. He could feel it in the pit of his stomach.

She stood by the door, watching first the boy and then him.

"My name is Lissa Hart. Sammy Lawson was my sister. Well, foster sister."

Sammy. He unsaddled the horse and led the animal to a stall to be dealt with later. He wouldn't put a horse out to pasture without giving it a good brushing and grain. Even a horse that had tossed him in the dirt.

It had been about six years since he'd seen Sammy. The mention of her had taken him back to a time and place, a version of himself, he'd rather forget. He needed a minute to collect his thoughts, so he made sure the horse had plenty of hay and fresh water. Finally, he turned to face Lissa Hart.

"Sammy? I haven't heard from her in a long time."

Pain sparked in her eyes and she blinked a few times. "Marcus, Sammy passed away. A little over a year ago. I thought you would have heard."

He walked away from her. Now he needed more than a minute. His heart constricted, reminding him he did indeed have one. Sammy gone. It didn't make sense. The two of them had dated for a few months until she broke it off with him. He hadn't loved her, but he had cared for her. They'd been a bad fit, in different places, rubbing each other wrong. She, like so many women in his life, had wanted more than a broken-down, dysfunctional bull rider with an alcohol problem.

It seemed like a lifetime ago.

Emotions in check, he faced her again. "What happened?"

"She had an accident. Her injuries were serious. I made it to the hospital, but…"

She closed her eyes and he understood.

"I'm sorry," he said more softly than normal, and his eyes misted with unwelcome dampness. "I tried to call her after she ended it with me. She let me know she didn't want me around."

"She had ideas about what she wanted in life."

"And it wasn't a rough bull rider from Bluebonnet Springs, Texas." He couldn't keep the resentment from his voice.

"She told me she was afraid together you'd be combustible and you'd self-destruct. She needed peace."

"Yeah, I get that. That brings us to why you're here, and then you can leave." He got the sneaking suspicion it wasn't going to go that way.

She swallowed hard, and he felt a pang of something resembling guilt or regret. She'd lost someone she considered a sister. Sammy had been young and so full of life. She'd had dreams. And now she was gone. He muttered under his breath and wiped his eyes. Contrary to how he was acting, he wasn't heartless.

"I'm here because she wanted me to find you."

"Find me why?" He took a step toward her and then changed direction so that he could look out the door, needing to check for himself that the boy was okay.

"He's your son." The words sprang from her lips, and for a minute he couldn't make sense of them.

The boy sat where they'd left him. He was making motor noises for his car and intent on building a ramp. Marcus watched him for a moment and then turned to face the woman who had just upended his entire world.

"No." He said it again. "No. She would have told me."

"She knew you weren't ready to settle down or ready for a family. She wanted to protect him the way she hadn't been protected as a child."

"Then why are you here now?"

"Because I promised." Her words were soft,

sad. She shrugged. "She had heard you were changing, getting your act together."

"That doesn't explain anything."

Her gaze dropped, but not before he saw the sheen of moisture. "I was with her at the hospital, and she told me to find you, and if you had your life together, then I should bring Oliver to meet you."

"You waited a year."

"I had to find you. I also had to keep my promise that I would make sure you had changed."

"You waited a year," he repeated, more angry than he'd been in a long time.

"I won't let anyone or anything hurt Oliver," she informed him. "And you haven't exactly been a model citizen."

That wasn't untrue. He gave her a steady look and wondered if she would back down. She didn't. He gave her points for that—most people didn't hold up under the glare he'd perfected since childhood.

"The kid is out there alone. You should go get him. And you should leave."

"The *kid* has a name. His name is Oliver and he's your son."

His son. He gave his head a quick shake. He had a son. The kid out there who had looked up at him with a mixture of fear, awe and concern was his. And he was the last person that boy needed in his life.

Lissa cleared her throat, gaining his attention.

"We have to finish this. And just because you go all angry cowboy on me doesn't mean I'm leaving. Sammy had a will. She gave me custody of Oliver. She wanted you in your son's life. But she had stipulations."

"I'm not good at ultimatums."

One shoulder lifted in a casual shrug. "I told her you wouldn't be happy about this."

She walked back to the door of the barn and peeked out.

"I think saying I'm not happy is an understatement. She kept my son from me. I'll admit I'm not looking to have a family, but I think a man should know when he has a child. At the very least I should have been helping out, supporting him." A light came on as those words left his mouth. "Oh. Is that why you're here?"

"For money?" In her defense, she looked pretty insulted. "I don't need your money. I brought Oliver to meet you because Sammy had some misguided notion that you would maybe grow up. I guess you told her often enough while you were dating that you didn't plan on being a husband or a father, but she thought you might change your mind."

He grabbed the brush out of a bucket and opened the stall door. The horse moved to his side, and he snapped a lead rope on the halter and led the animal to the cross ties in the center of the barn. He needed something to focus on, something other than the obvious. He was a father. The role he least wanted in life was now his.

He pretended it was anger he felt, but a good dose of fear got mixed up in the emotion. Fear of failing a child. Fear of being like his own father.

"I'm not responsible. I doubt I ever will be. So I guess you ought to take the kid and go." If he acted as if he didn't care, maybe she would believe him and leave. Maybe she would take the boy and give him a chance at a happier, healthier life than either Sammy or Marcus had known growing up.

"Go where?" the boy asked from the open door of the barn.

Marcus stroked the brush down the gelding's neck. Once. Twice. Three times. With each stroke of the brush, he took a deep breath. And then he eased around to face the little boy. Oliver. *His son.*

Because of his own father, he recognized himself in that little boy. He saw a kid who was unsure. He saw fear. He saw uncertainty. He had been that kid. And now he was the dad. He hadn't planned on being a parent because he'd never wanted to see that look in a kid's eyes.

His attention shifted from the boy to the aunt. She didn't believe in him. The fact that he cared what she thought was his third surprise of the day and none of those surprises had really been pleasant.

Lissa Hart held out her hand and Oliver hurried to her side. His small hand tucked into hers and she gave it a gentle squeeze. She didn't know what else to say to Marcus Palermo. While she certainly hadn't expected this to be easy, she found it even harder than she'd imagined.

Something about this man made her uneasy. Not afraid. She didn't think he would hurt Oliver. He seemed rough and unfeeling, but she'd seen something in his expression, in the depths of his dark eyes, that told her he felt plenty.

Sammy had fancied herself in love with Marcus, but she'd ended the relationship because he was too broken, too angry to be the kind of person she could count on. Still, her sister had wanted him to heal, and she'd wanted him to have a chance with his son.

He'd stopped brushing the horse and he focused on Oliver, his dark gaze studying the little boy, a miniature version of himself. His mouth twitched, as if he might have found humor in something. The movement drew her attention to the jagged scar across his left cheek. That scar did nothing to detract from his looks. His too-long hair curling at his collar gave him a youthful appearance. But the firm jawline, the not-quite smile on his lips— those belonged to a man. A man who had lived a hard life and seen a lot of pain.

He shifted his focus from Oliver to her, and one brow arched in what could only be a challenge. She didn't flinch or look away. Neither did he, but then he dismissed her and returned his attention to Oliver. He squatted, holding out the brush.

"Do you want to brush him before you leave?" he asked quietly.

Oliver nodded because he was a little boy and of course he wanted to stand by this cowboy and brush the horse. He looked up at Lissa, seeking permission. He didn't know yet that this man was his father. She hadn't known how to tell him, and she hadn't wanted him to be disappointed. The odds had been good that Marcus would reject his child or not be able to be a parent to him, and her main goal was to protect Oliver. Sammy had entrusted her with his care.

With Marcus watching, Lissa let go of Oliver's hand and the boy slipped away from her. Her heart clenched in agony as she realized this might be the beginning of losing the child she loved so very much.

Oliver took the brush and Marcus lifted him, telling him to run the brush down the horse's neck.

"Put pressure on it," he said, in that gruff whisper of a voice, "or it tickles and horses don't like to be tickled." Oliver grinned at that and pushed the brush down the horse's neck.

Marcus continued to hold Oliver. He spoke quietly to his son, words that Lissa couldn't hear.

Tempted as she was to move closer, she stood there, waiting. He seemed content to ignore her and focus on Oliver. The two looked like father and son, dark heads together as Oliver leaned close to hug the horse.

"I think we can turn him out to pasture," Marcus said as he returned Oliver to the ground.

"And we should finish our discussion," she inserted.

"There's an old tire swing," Marcus told Oliver. "Want to try it out?"

"Is it safe?" Lissa asked.

"It's safe." Leading the horse to the door at

the rear of the barn, he opened it and turned the horse loose. He stood there a moment, a dark silhouette against the sun, as the horse trotted a short distance away and then dropped to roll on the ground. A cloud of dust billowed around the big horse as he stood and shook like a dog. Next to her, Oliver laughed at the sight.

Marcus once again faced them, his expression still and composed. He held out a hand to Oliver. "Let's go check out that swing."

Lissa followed them outside into bright May sunshine. The house that lay a short distance from the barn was an older farmhouse, two stories with a long front porch. Beyond the house was a creek, the waters sparkling and clear.

The homestead looked a bit run-down, with faded siding, patched sections on the roof and a board over one window. It could have been any house she'd known growing up in poor neighborhoods, but instead it seemed peaceful. Maybe it was the location, with the stream, the rosebushes that had taken over and the green fields in the distance.

Thinking about the house pulled her back to her own troubled past, to the abuse with her drug-addicted mother. Life before foster care and the Simms family. She and Sammy had lived their teen years with Tom and Jane Simms.

"It took me a while to find you," she told him as they walked in the direction of a big tree with limbs that stretched out like an umbrella, shading the yard of the old house.

"That's the whole idea, being hard to find."

He helped Oliver onto the swing and gave it a push. "We're going to sit on the porch. You'll be okay here."

Oliver grinned big. "It's fun here."

"Yeah, it is." He gave the boy one last look and headed for the house.

He didn't turn back to see if she followed. Lissa tried not to let that hurt. She wasn't here for herself. But it mattered, whether or not he was good and if he was caring. Oliver needed a real father, someone to look up to. Someone who would be there for him.

She stepped onto the front porch and glanced around. It needed paint and a few boards had to be repaired. There were chairs and an old dog sleeping in a worn-out dog bed. The animal lifted his head to give them a once-over.

"Lucky isn't much of a guard dog," Marcus told her as he pointed to a chair. "He's been following me around the country for the past ten years. He's half-deaf and nearly blind."

Lissa thought the dog was a piece of the puzzle that was Marcus Palermo. The black-and-brown hound dog fixed soulful eyes on his master and then her. They must not have appeared too interesting, because he yawned and fell back to sleep.

"Why is his name Lucky?"

"He got hit by a car when he was a puppy. I found him on the side of the road and nursed him back to health and he's been Lucky ever since," Marcus explained as he sat on the edge of the porch. "About the boy. Are you dumping him here, like he's a stray? Or do you want money?"

"He is not a stray. He's a little boy and I love him. I'm here to see if you're ready to be a part of his life."

"You make it sound like I was given a choice and rejected him."

"Sammy gave me the job of making sure you are ready to be a dad."

"Make sure I'm ready?" A cold thread of anger sharpened the words. He was no longer the easygoing cowboy he'd been moments ago. When she looked up, his gaze was on her, as glacial as his words.

"Sammy didn't know if you would want to be a father. She also didn't know if you would be able."

"I see. I guess I do have more negatives than positives. Bad-tempered, dysfunctional and a recovering drunk. Not much hope in all of that."

"She loved her son and wanted him safe." Lissa didn't add that she wanted Oliver safe. She wanted to protect him and make sure his future was secure.

"So you think I should have to jump through your hoops in order to be his dad? Because the way I see it, I could just take you to court."

She knew that, but on hearing him say it, emotion rolled through her, settling in the pit of her stomach and making her heart ache. Her gaze settled on Oliver as he worked to keep the swing moving.

"It would be unfair to Oliver to do this without taking time to allow him to get to know you. To bond with you. I need to know that you're responsible and that you'll be a good dad."

"You need to make sure I'm not my father," he said without animosity, as if he was removed from the situation with his father, a known cult leader.

"Okay. Yes. And I do have legal custody."

"I'm going to be honest here. I don't think you should leave him with me." He glanced her way and then his attention turned to Oliver. "He seems like a good kid. Anyone in their right mind would want him. I know *you* want him. And, well, I don't want to mess that little boy up. He's already had it rough. Why make things worse for him?"

"Because he's yours," she pointed out. "Because he deserves to know he has a father."

"Not everyone knows how to be a father. Some people don't deserve the title."

Marcus watched as the little boy got off the swing, gave it a push and then struggled to climb back on the moving tire. The dog suddenly took interest in his surroundings and the visitors. He stood, shook from head to toe and trotted off the porch and across the yard to Oliver.

The rangy old dog, some type of coon dog, she guessed, obviously held more appeal than the swing. Oliver jumped, rolled across the ground and then giggled as the animal licked his face.

"Lucky. Enough." Marcus whistled. The dog stopped licking, but he didn't return to the porch. Instead, he plopped on his belly and stretched out next to his new friend.

"You should give yourself a chance." She found herself uttering the last words she'd wanted to say to him.

He scoffed. "No, I don't think so. Give myself a chance to what? Mess that kid up? He's happy. Let's keep it that way."

"Don't you want him to know that you're his dad?"

He pushed himself to his feet and leaned against the post. "No. I don't want him to know. I'm sure you know plenty about my family. I told myself a long time ago that I wouldn't be a part of continuing the family line."

"And yet you did. That little boy is your family."

"And he's got you. You look like a perfectly normal, responsible adult, and you love him. If it's money you're worried about, he isn't going to go without. I'll make sure of that."

She glared at him. "Money doesn't replace a parent or parents, Mr. Palermo."

He met her gaze with a fiery look of his own. "I'm Marcus. Mr. Palermo was my father. And that's a good enough reason for you to take the boy and go."

She stood and walked past him, her shoulder brushing his. He didn't make a move to chase her down and stop her. She kind of wished he had, because she thought if he'd give himself a chance, he had a shot at being a good dad.

Oliver resisted when she told him they had to leave, but Marcus Palermo had already gone inside. What kind of man could turn his back and walk away without even offering a good-bye to his child? She knew the answer. A man who had been damaged, just as Sammy had warned. A man who didn't want to look too closely at what he was turning his back on.

She considered pounding on his door, demanding he care. But a person couldn't be forced to care. She'd learned that lesson at an early age.

Chapter Two

The next morning, Marcus woke with regrets. He stumbled to the kitchen and poured water into the coffeemaker before heading out the back door to the one thing he'd actually done to the old farmhouse. He'd added a porch with a swing, and he spent many a morning there watching the sun come up.

Nothing said *home* like a porch swing.

He loved the start of a new day when the sky turned from inky black to gray, and then that big orange ball peeked up from the horizon, the colors bursting forth like God sweeping a whole handful of crayons across the sky. Not that he would have shared that thought with anyone. No one knew how he felt about faith or life or art.

Art, another of his ventures and something

he kept hidden in the upstairs bedroom, away from prying eyes.

He had a son. He had rejected the boy and it had cost him. Last night he'd lain awake thinking of that little boy's eyes, his face. He'd been a funny kid, rolling on the ground with Lucky. Marcus thought of his nieces, Issy and Jewel. With a sigh, he took a seat on the porch swing and buried his face in his hands. *Father, if it is Your will, take this cup from me.*

Jesus had uttered those words in the Garden of Gethsemane just before he was taken into custody. He guessed having a son didn't quite match up to what Jesus had been about to endure. But what Jesus had done had been the ultimate act of obedience, of giving himself up for others.

Marcus could admit to being torn. He had given his son up because he felt he wasn't the dad Oliver needed. He wasn't what any kid needed. It hadn't been easy to watch his son take hold of someone else's hand and walk away. Like a coward, he'd headed inside so he wouldn't have to meet the boy's dark and questioning eyes.

Oliver would be better off without him. He'd be better off with the woman, Lissa Hart. She seemed decent. She seemed to care. She would meet a good, honorable guy, get married, and they'd be a family. He'd meant to make himself feel better with the thought; instead, he felt worse. His son would be someone else's family.

He leaned back in the swing as the sun peeped up over the eastern horizon, and he called himself a fool. He knew better than anyone that appearances were an illusion. His dad had been the master of the game, creating a facade that fooled people until they were too far into his web to escape. His own family had been victims of the deception.

Jesse Palermo's wife, mother to his children, had preferred walking away from her own flesh and blood to staying with a madman. Marcus bore the scars of his dad's abuse—his broken voice, the jagged line down his cheek and the emotional baggage.

His sister Lucy and his twin, Alex, had worked through their pain and married. Their youngest sister, Maria, seemed to have survived. Only because she'd been a little girl when Jesse died.

Marcus had been drifting for the past ten years or so, since their illustrious sire had died on the back of a bull he'd challenged Alex to ride. Marcus had made some money, sowed his wild oats and done his best to outrun the past. And he had a son. A boy named Oliver. A boy who would be better off without Marcus, because the only thing Marcus knew about being a father was what his dad had taught him. Jesse Palermo had beaten his children. He'd controlled his family and his congregation. He'd ruined every life he'd come in contact with.

A car barreled down his drive, tossing up dust and invading the early-morning peacefulness. He groaned when he recognized the old International wagon. His aunt Essie's pride and joy. It wasn't quite seven in the morning, so he doubted this was a pleasure visit. He headed inside for whatever lecture happened to be forthcoming. His skin was thick and she'd told him on more than one occasion that so was his head.

She met him on the front porch. Knocking on the door to seventy, she was a spitfire with long, graying hair pulled back in a braid. Today she wore jeans, a T-shirt and her apron. She'd obviously been at the café she owned before heading to his house on whatever mission had brought her.

Marcus sighed. He wasn't fooling himself. He knew what had brought her out here. The same thing that had kept him up all night and had him doubting himself this morning.

"Aunt Essie, I just made coffee."

She had a spatula in her hand. She must have

carried it out of the café with her, but she went ahead and waved it in his face.

"You!" After decades in America, her Brazilian accent was normally undetectable, but today was a different story. "You've pulled stunts in your life, but *this*? Oh, I should paddle you, Marcus Palermo."

He drew in a breath and exhaled. She could only be talking about one thing. Or one person. "How'd you find out?"

"Yesterday afternoon Mindy rented a room above her store. The young woman showed up with a boy that looked a lot like you and Alex when you were little. This morning that young lady came in my café, and wasn't I surprised?" She waved the spatula a little too closely to his face. He grabbed it from her hand and tossed it onto the counter.

"Imagine my surprise when she showed up here," he countered.

"So you sent her on her way as if the boy, your flesh and blood, doesn't matter."

He recoiled at the way she described his decision and her eyes narrowed, as if she'd spotted a chink in his armor.

"What, Marcus, you don't want to take responsibility for your actions?" she demanded. She'd been more a parent to the Palermo offspring than their own mother and father, and he wasn't surprised by her questions. He wasn't even offended. Truth was, he did feel guilty.

"I sent her away because the boy does matter," he told her as he spun on his heel and walked back to the kitchen. "Coffee?"

"There you go, shutting yourself off, acting as if none of this concerns you. As if you don't have emotions."

"It concerns me," he said as he poured her a cup of coffee. She took it and gave him a long look. "What about this concerns you?"

Wrong thing to say. He knew it when she moved closer, her lips thinning with displeasure.

"What concerns me is that there is a boy in need of a father and you're acting as if it isn't your responsibility."

"I'll support him. I'll give him whatever he needs."

"But not your time. Or your love. The two most important things you can give a child." She started to ramble in Portuguese, which he spoke little of.

He poured coffee in his favorite mug and tried to ignore the memories that the cup evoked. He hadn't even thought about it when he'd pulled it from the cabinet. Sammy had given him the mug with the verse from Lamentations, about God's mercy being new every morning. She'd wanted him to remember that each day was a fresh canvas. He guessed that might be one reason he loved mornings. They did feel new. A fresh start. Every day.

New, even though the old baggage kind of held on and wasn't easy to be rid of.

It bugged him that he'd pulled that mug out of the cabinet. He looked up, wondering if God was telling him something and wishing He hadn't bothered.

"He's your son, Marcus. That's as clear as that ugly nose on your face." Aunt Essie had resumed English, like someone had pushed a switch.

"My nose isn't ugly," he replied. "And that boy deserves better than a dad who might or might not be his own father's son. I won't do that to any woman or any child. That's why Sammy kept him from me. I don't know why she made the decision to have his guardian introduce him to me after she was gone."

A wash of grief flooded him, bringing the sting of tears to his eyes that he'd regret later. Aunt Essie's expression softened and she put a hand on his arm, giving a light squeeze.

"I'm sorry. I'm sure you cared about her." Essie patted his arm. "You are Jesse Palermo's son, but that doesn't mean you are going to be the same kind of father he was. You are your own person. And if there was good in him, I prefer to think that's what you have in you. My nephew wasn't a bad man. Power and alcohol changed him."

He closed his eyes, willing away the dampness. He didn't cry. His dad had beat the tears out of him years ago with the old phrase that he'd give him something to cry about. After a few good, sound beatings, he'd no longer cared to find something to cry about.

"I did care about her, but together we were combustible. It wasn't a good thing, the two of us. Two kids with similar pasts and a lot of anger. We were both getting our acts together. She was further along that path and she didn't want to be pulled backward."

"Okay, so the two of you didn't work. That isn't the boy's fault. The woman is at the café with the boy, Oliver. And I refuse to let you throw this away. He's your son. He needs you." She gave him a quick hug. "And I think you need him. You have ten minutes to get your act together and get to town."

She left with one last warning to do the right thing. He'd tried to tell her that yesterday he'd done the right thing. He'd sent Oliver off to live a life with a woman who obviously loved him. A woman who seemed to know how to be a parent.

A woman who had sparked something foreign inside Marcus. She'd looked at him with those sky blue eyes of hers, and she, too, had challenged him to do the right thing. And he'd wanted to.

Which resulted in the decision he'd made. He'd sent her on her way. But she hadn't left town. Why hadn't she left? Because she was stubborn, that was why. Because for some reason she thought he should be involved in Oliver's life. For what purpose?

Thunder rumbled in the distance and gray clouds rolled from the south. He'd seen the forecast and knew they were in for some serious rain. The kind of rain that could only cause trouble. It seemed that the weather was the least of his concerns. He had to get to town and convince Lissa Hart to leave.

He didn't want himself tied to the woman. That was another good reason to send her back to where she came from. Having Oliver in his life clearly meant having Lissa there, as well. If one was trouble, the two together was catastrophe. As if on cue, lightning flashed across the sky.

The rain started as Lissa stood with her cell phone on the covered porch of Essie's café.

Her mom, or foster mom, Jane Simms, continued to talk.

"You have to give him a chance." Jane was repeating what she'd already said more than once. "Oliver is his son. And it will be easier if you honor Sammy's wishes. If he comes back later and takes you to court, well, you don't want that for Oliver."

"No, I don't."

"You have vacation time. It wouldn't hurt you to take time off."

The wind blew the rain across the porch, the drops pelting Lissa's face. She wiped away the moisture and glanced inside the café, where Oliver was digging into his biscuits and gravy. He waved happily.

"I know and I need the time off, for more reasons than this."

"Is he still calling you?" Jane asked, speaking of a fellow nurse Lissa had dated for a short time.

"Not as often." She wanted to cry over the entire situation, but that wasn't her style. She would work through this, because on the scale of disasters she'd faced in her lifetime, this definitely didn't rate highest.

"His problems aren't yours," Jane reminded.

"I know. It's Troy's past that is the problem. And my past." She had fallen for a smile and sweeping romantic gestures, not realizing the baggage that came with both.

"It's okay to have goals, Lis. It's okay to want more. And it is okay to stay here and give this man a chance with his son. You're a good judge of character. That's why Sammy trusted you to know if he was ready to be a dad."

"I don't really want this responsibility. I love Oliver. I don't want to hurt him, and regardless of how I go with this, that could happen."

"But no matter what happens, you'll protect him," Jane countered. "I know you will. You've been more than an aunt to that little boy since the day he was born."

She sighed, holding the phone tight to her ear as thunder rumbled across a sky heavy with clouds. It was May. Of course there would be storms.

Neither she nor her foster mom spoke for several long moments. As much as they had loved Sammy, they'd also known her faults. She had struggled, even after Oliver's birth. Neither of them wanted to speak of the past, not when it meant dwelling on the Sammy who had slipped into old behaviors and left her son too often with Jane or Lissa.

She'd been trying to straighten up and do right. That was what they focused on. She'd been working so hard on being better, for Oliver's sake.

"Don't dwell on it," Jane spoke softly. "You've taken a lot on yourself. And Sammy left a large hole in your life, along with this burden. You know I'm praying for you."

"I know you are." She looked anxiously up at the sky again. "I'd better let you go. It's raining harder and making it difficult to hear. I'm going to go back inside with Oliver."

"Give him kisses from his Gee Gee."

Lissa smiled as she said goodbye and she felt better. Jane always made her feel better. She was a true mother, even if she had come late to Lissa's life. Her own mother had failed Lissa for the first fourteen years, but Jane and Tom Simms had picked up the pieces and given her a future. They were the parents she turned to. Her own mother was someone she occasionally reached out to, hoping to find her better.

As she entered the restaurant, the wind picked up and so did the rain. Big drops splattered the windows and bounced off the cars parked along the front of Essie's. A flash of lightning lit up the early-morning sky and Oliver gulped as he swallowed a bite of biscuits and gravy. Wide-eyed, he looked up at Lissa as she sat down across from him.

"Is it a tornado?" he asked in hushed tones.

"No," she assured him. "Just rain. We always need rain in the spring."

A woman ran out of the kitchen. "Land sakes, it's gonna flood. I heard it on the news."

The waitress hurried from a table where she'd just delivered an order and took the older woman by the hand. "Bea, it isn't a flood. It's a storm. We get them in the spring and they pass. Look, there's a little boy and you don't want to scare him. Head on back to the kitchen. I left an order for you to cook while Essie is gone."

The woman, midfifties and wearing a floral-print dress, orthopedic shoes and athletic socks, focused her wild-eyed attention on Oliver. Her lips pursed and her eyes narrowed.

"Why, doesn't he look the spittin' image of the Palermo twins? I reckon someone is in big trouble and that's why Essie went roaring out of here in her old Scout. She said Marcus was about to get his ears boxed."

The waitress tugged on the woman's arm. "Bea, back to the kitchen."

Bea remained standing, wringing her hands in her apron. She glanced at Oliver and then at the windows. Lightning flashed across the sky. She trembled visibly.

"Is the little boy scared?" Bea asked the waitress, Libby. "I remember Marcus and Alex hiding under tables when it stormed. They were little like that."

"He isn't afraid." Libby tried to move the cook, but Bea wouldn't budge.

The bells chimed, signaling that the café door had opened. A breeze too cool for mid-May swept through the café and the rain became a deafening roar. Lissa didn't have to look to know who would be coming through the door. She knew because the woman, Bea, glanced from the door to Oliver and back to the door. She knew because Oliver stopped looking worried and grinned big.

"I'm going back to the kitchen," Bea announced. "Marcus is in big trouble."

Marcus nodded a greeting to a few people, pulled off his hat and headed in their direction. He half grinned at Oliver as he pulled out the empty chair at their table.

"Mind if I sit?" he asked as he folded his lean, athletic frame into the seat. He'd taken off his hat and he dropped it on Oliver's head.

Lissa started to ask if it mattered that she did mind. Instead, she forced a smile and shook her head. "No. Of course not."

At her terse response he grinned and nodded at the coffee cup on the table. He turned the cup over for the waitress to fill and leaned back as if he didn't feel the tension. But even

Oliver felt it. The boy glanced from Marcus to Lissa and back to Marcus.

"Are you enjoying your biscuits and gravy?" he asked Oliver.

"Yeah. They're the best." Oliver took another big bite. "Can I see your dog again?"

"Maybe," he answered.

Lissa wanted to hurt him for being so noncommittal. She wanted to yell at him for invading their lives and turning everything upside down. But then, hadn't she been the one doing the invading? Because she'd made this trip, none of their lives would ever be the same.

"Hey, Oliver, want to come back to the kitchen and help me make today's dessert? You can even taste the pudding to make sure it's good." Essie, owner of the café and Marcus's aunt, approached their table. She wiped her hands on her apron and appeared to be completely innocent of interfering.

"Can I?" Oliver looked from Essie to Lissa. And then his gaze drifted to Marcus, and for the first time the boy seemed confused and unsure of the situation. "Aunt Lissa, are you okay?"

"Of course I'm okay. And yes, you can go with Miss Essie. I think that would be fun. When you get back, we'll leave."

He gave her a quick hug, and the feel of his

small arms wrapping around her neck was the sweetest thing ever. He wasn't hers, but she loved him as if he were. Marcus Palermo could take him from her. She'd known that when she came here. She'd known for the past year that her time with Oliver might be limited. It had been a constant source of stress.

Essie gave them both a long look that held a lot of meaning, then she walked off with Oliver's hand tucked in hers. The two were discussing chocolate pie and brownies. Oliver glanced back as he walked through the door to the kitchen.

"Surprise," Marcus whispered as the doors to the kitchen closed. They weren't alone. There were still people in the café sending them curious looks that they didn't try to disguise.

"Yes. I didn't expect to see you this morning."

"Imagine how I felt when my aunt showed up at my place to inform me there was a woman in town and she had a little boy that looks a lot like me. Why are you still in town?"

He had a point. A good one. "I couldn't leave. I wanted you to have a night to think about Oliver and being a father."

"So you planned on giving me another

chance?" He arched a brow at her, clearly questioning her honesty. Or her sanity.

Lissa didn't quite know what to say.

She had wanted to go on, to forget Marcus and Bluebonnet Springs. But Oliver had been in the back seat of the car, his dark eyes intent on her face in the mirror, and he'd asked about Marcus and wondered if he'd been a friend of his mommy. Pushing aside her feelings of protectiveness, for Oliver's sake she'd searched for a place to stay. For one night, she'd told herself. To give Marcus a chance.

She didn't want to get ten years down the road and have Oliver ask her why she'd kept him from his father. She also didn't want to settle into her life as Oliver's mom and have Marcus show up out of the blue one day and take him.

"You could give a guy a chance to catch his breath. This did come out of nowhere," Marcus said. The admission seemed pulled from deep inside. "It's hard for me to imagine Sammy keeping this from me. I know we weren't a good match. But he's mine. That's pretty obvious."

"So, does a new day make things different for you?"

"His mercies are new every morning." He spoke so softly she almost didn't hear the words she hadn't expected from this hardened cowboy. "Nothing is different. But everything has changed."

"Meaning?"

"I don't know how to be a father. I didn't plan on getting married or bringing kids into the world."

"You can't undo what already is." Her heart ached for the little boy who at that moment was eating pudding and didn't know that his father was sitting there trying to figure out if he could be a part of his life.

He toyed with the spoon next to his coffee cup. "It isn't that I don't want him. But I don't want to hurt him. He's better off with you."

"He's your son."

He sat there for a long minute looking at her. "Right. My son that Sammy didn't tell me about. That speaks volumes."

"She was afraid."

"Of me." One brow arched. She understood what he meant. Sammy had given birth to his son and then decided he wasn't suitable to be in his child's life. And later she'd regretted that decision.

Meeting him changed everything for Lissa. She hadn't expected to like him. She hadn't expected a lot of things about him. Like his thoughtfulness. Or the depth of emotion in his dark eyes.

"Time goes by and what seemed like a good decision starts to look like a bad one. Sammy regretted not telling you. And then she ran out of time." She closed her eyes to regroup. It had been a year. She still missed her friend. Her sister. "And now you're about to make the same mistake. What looks like a good idea today, five years down the road, might be the worst mistake of your life."

"Valid point," he said. "But if I allow you to tell him I'm his father, and I hurt him… Five years down the road, we can't undo the damage. Speaking from experience, that kind of hurt can't be undone."

She wasn't here to share stories, but she understood the damage an abusive parent could do to a child. She understood the scars, invisible and visible.

She understood how it affected relationships.

"You should at least get to know him."

"How would that work, me getting to know him? How would you explain to him who I am and why he is spending time with me?"

"I'm not sure. We don't have to tell him you're his dad. Not until you're ready. Or until we think he is ready."

She glanced toward the window. The sky

had darkened and, if possible, the rain came down harder.

"This rain is only getting worse."

He was right. The rain was coming down in sheets. After the previous week of rain, she knew that the creeks would rise. The roads back to San Antonio would be a nightmare.

Before she left, she had to put all of her cards on the table. He deserved the whole truth, even if it meant losing Oliver. She reached into her purse and pulled out the letter.

"You should read this. Sammy left it with her will."

He took the paper, but he didn't open it. Instead, he slipped it into his pocket. "I'll look at it some other time."

"Sooner rather than later, Marcus."

"Right."

"Fine, here's my number." She wrote it on a napkin and handed it to him.

Thunder crashed and the windows rattled with the force of the wind. He glanced at her number and back to the storm raging outside. "You might ought to stay in town."

"I'll be fine. It's just a little rain. And it might let up before I leave. I have to pack up and check out of our room at the B and B."

She stood to retrieve Oliver from the kitchen,

but Marcus pushed himself out of his chair first. "I'll get him."

It was a start, so she waited where she stood and watched as he headed for the kitchen.

He had stories. She didn't want them. She didn't want to be affected by a man her foster sister had deemed "too broken." She'd always had a soft spot for broken things. It was her reason for becoming a nurse. Because as a nurse she had a reason to care, a reason to fix broken people. Fix them and send them home. Once she sent them home, they were out of her life. And then she had new people to care about, to help.

Lissa knew her own hang-ups. She had lived in a broken and abusive home with a mother who never put her child first. A mother she had tried to fix. And she'd failed. Time and again. Six months ago she had promised herself that she wouldn't be used. Ever again. She wouldn't enable. She wouldn't give money. She would always care—she would pray for the woman who had given her life—but she wouldn't give her the power to hurt her.

She and Sammy had been from similar backgrounds. As teens in the Simms home, they had made a pact to never be abused again, or tie themselves to broken men who would wound them the way their own mothers had been wounded. And they wouldn't have children with men who would leave scars.

When Sammy had met Marcus, she'd been drawn to him in a way she'd deemed unhealthy. She'd never introduced him to Lissa, but she'd told her about him and about how easy it had been to fall for his charm. She'd lost herself a little, and when she realized that, she'd broken things off.

A few minutes later Marcus returned with Oliver. His aunt stood in the doorway of the kitchen, her mouth a firm line of disapproval. Marcus squatted, putting himself at eye level with his son. Lissa watched, wondering if Oliver suspected that this man was his father.

"You be good, okay?" Marcus said. She heard the rasp of emotion and knew he cared. That he cared spoke well of him. If only he realized that.

"I'll be good. Can I come back and see your dog?" Oliver took a slight step forward. "And could I get a hat like yours?"

Marcus nodded and he looked up, meeting her gaze. He stood and backed up a step, putting a hand on his son's head.

"We'll be in touch?" Lissa asked.

Again he nodded. She took Oliver by the hand and left. Even though he'd said they would be in touch, she wondered if he meant to keep his word or if this was an easy way to say goodbye.

Chapter Three

A couple of hours after saying goodbye to Lissa and Oliver, Marcus was in the field, feeling thankful for a break in the clouds and for the help of his twin.

"How much rain are we supposed to get?" Marcus asked Alex as the two of them moved cattle from twenty acres along the creek to higher ground. They had opted for ATVs over horses. The rain had slacked off for a short time and they wanted to get the job done as quickly as possible.

"They're saying up to a foot of rain toward the weekend. This is just the appetizer," Alex responded as he moved his four-wheeler the opposite direction in order to keep a few steers from bolting back toward the creek.

Marcus glanced in the direction of his house. If they got that much rain, his house would be under water. The creek was coming up fast. He had sandbags, but he knew he couldn't control the rise of water if there was a flash flood.

"We'll do what we can to keep the water out," Alex called out as they moved the cattle through the open gate.

A cow spooked. Marcus went after her, turning the four-wheeler hard to the right to stop her. She moved back to the herd and Alex closed the gate behind her. As they headed for the barn, the rain started again. They hit the throttles and raced side by side, stopping after they'd reached the safety of the equipment barn.

Alex was laughing as he climbed from the four-wheeler. He took off his hat and shook it. "Wow, this makes a guy want to build an ark."

Marcus shrugged out of his raincoat. "I hate rain."

"But you hate it more when we're going through a drought and everything dries up." Alex sat sideways on the seat of the ATV. "So, when are you going to tell me about your kid?"

"I guess I kind of thought it wasn't any of your business."

"Really? I'm your brother. Your twin. It seems to me I'd be the person most likely to listen if you need to talk. You had to know that everyone in town would be talking about how much that little boy looks like you."

"I guess I hadn't thought about it. And no need to analyze my mental condition, brother, I'm fine."

"Of course you're fine. But you have a son. That's huge."

"Yeah, it is." He sat there thinking about Oliver. "He seems like a pretty great kid. And I don't want to mess that up for him."

"I get that. But we don't always get to choose how things work out," Alex responded. "Well, we should make a run for the house before the rain picks up again."

"You can head home. I'll do the rest of this myself. I'm sure you want to see Marissa." Alex's wife of five months. He'd found her standing on the side of the road in a wedding dress. She was a little bitty thing, but fierce, and she'd convinced Alex to give up his single ways. They'd married in December, a year after they'd first met.

Alex wasn't Marcus. As kids they'd been different as night and day. The same went for the two of them as adults. Alex thought things out and let things go. Marcus had always battled it out and held on to his anger. When it came to their father, Alex had tried to reason. He'd searched to find ways to solve their problems. Conversely, Marcus had gone at Jesse and he'd paid physically for his efforts.

Marcus's phone buzzed. He glanced at the unfamiliar number and answered. "Marcus Palermo."

"Marcus, Guy Phipps here. We've got a car in the ditch just south of the old crossroads bridge."

"Who is it?" He glanced at his brother. Alex had moved closer, pulling out his phone as he did. Probably worrying about his wife. Or their sister Lucy. Even Maria, if she was on her way home from college. She'd begun her summer break just a few days ago and planned on heading home.

"Not from around here. Name is…" Guy paused. "Name's Lissa Hart. She's got a little boy with her. She said to call you."

He took a deep breath and made eye contact with Alex, who now appeared worried. "Are they hurt?"

"Nothing serious. Doc is here. He's checking her shoulder. The little guy might have bumped his head." Guy paused again. In the background, Marcus heard sirens.

It shook him. Marcus could willingly get on the biggest and meanest bulls in the country, a ton of pure rage and power. It might get his adrenaline going, but it didn't shake him.

It didn't make him feel weak as a kitten and helpless to do anything.

"Guy, are they taking them to the hospital? Do I need to meet them somewhere?" Marcus glanced at Alex, who had followed as he walked away, wanting privacy, wanting to put on a mask, as if this didn't matter. Alex wore a worried expression and Marcus knew his own would match. The two of them might be different, but they were the same. The twin thing wasn't just a myth.

He knew Alex would feel his concern. And from that troubled look in his dark eyes, Marcus understood Alex felt his brother's guilt. He'd sent the kid away. He didn't know how to be a dad, so he had sent his son on down the road in the middle of a torrential rainstorm with floods predicted. Proof that he didn't deserve to be a parent. He wasn't any better than his own father, putting his own feelings ahead of the safety of a child.

And Lissa. He hadn't given her a second thought once he'd said his goodbyes. At least, he'd told himself he wasn't going to give her a second thought. It counted, that he'd intended to forget her. But even now, those blue eyes of hers triggered a memory. She'd challenged him to care. For his son.

Few people got away with challenging him. Few people had the backbone for it.

On the other end of the line the first responder was giving him information. He had to focus. "Doc said he's going to drive them back to his office if you want to meet him there. The boy is asking for you. He's a tough kid." There was a smile in the first responder's voice.

"Put him on the phone." Marcus waited and pretty soon a hiccup over the phone told him Oliver was there and fighting tears. "Hey, little man. You okay?"

"I hit my head."

"I bet that hurt."

"It did. They said I wasn't uncon...uncon..." He sounded like a boy trying to be brave.

"Unconscious?" Marcus supplied.

"Yeah. So I'm okay."

"Nothing else hurts?"

"Nope," Oliver said on a sniffle.

"Is Lissa okay?"

More sniffling and then, "Yeah, I think. She says her shoulder hurts. She's not crying, though. Doc said she's tougher than a bull rider. I think you're a bull rider."

"I am a bull rider," Marcus told his son. *His son.* "Listen, I'm going to see you in a few minutes. You're tough. You've got this."

"Yeah, I'm tough." The boy sounded like he meant to convince himself.

"I'll be there in a few minutes, so you keep being tough and you take care of Lissa. She's not as tough as she's pretending to be."

He ended the call.

"Let's go," Alex said. "I'll drive."

"I can drive. I want to grab a couple of blankets from the house." Marcus headed for his truck.

"They're fine," Alex called out to him. "If they were in bad shape, Doc would send them to Killeen."

"I know that." Marcus opened his truck door and found his keys in the ignition. Alex climbed in on the other side.

"You should take your keys out."

"Yeah, I know. But spare me the lectures."

"So you don't want me to tell you that you care about this kid and you shouldn't let him walk away?" Alex reached to turn up the heat.

"I want you to stay out of my business."

Alex gave him a thumbs-up. "Right."

"Don't talk."

His twin zipped his lips.

Marcus might have grinned at the ridiculous gesture, but he didn't have an ounce of humor in him. He had sent his kid away in this weather. His reckless decision had put Oliver and Lissa in danger.

It took fifteen minutes to get to the scene of the accident.

Flashing lights and scattered emergency vehicles lined the road. Marcus pulled behind a first responder and got out. The rain had picked back up. He saw Lissa sitting in Doc Parker's car. Oliver sat huddled against her, his face pale and a bandage over the right side of his forehead. Doc leaned in talking to them.

The car she'd been driving now sat on the back of a tow truck. The driver's side was dented and the tires on the passenger's side were flat. Alex said something to him about seeing where they would tow the car.

When Marcus appeared behind Doc, Oliver noticed first and big tears rolled down his cheeks. Marcus pushed away memories of his sister looking much the same way. He hadn't been able to help Lucy, but he could help Oliver. At least for today he could handle things and make sure the child wasn't frightened and didn't feel alone.

And then he made eye contact with Lissa and he could see in her blue eyes that she was being strong for Oliver. He recognized the flicker of pain that flashed across her features, tightening the lines around her mouth. But she managed a smile as she raised her left hand in a half-hearted wave.

"The roads are a mess," she informed him with a hint of humor in her voice.

"Yeah, I've heard." He leaned against the side of the car. "How are they, Doc?"

"Oh, not too bad all things considered. I think Miss Hart has a dislocated shoulder. Actually, she's a nurse and that's her diagnosis. I would concur. Mr. Oliver has a good bump on his head, but I think he's okay. I'll take them back to my office. We'll get that shoulder back in place and I'll turn them over to you."

Turn them over to him? He started to object. He was the last person they should be relying on. But Oliver looked happy with the news. And Lissa Hart looked...relieved?

Lissa kept her left arm around Oliver. Her right arm she kept at her side. Every bump jostled it and sent a shooting pain to her shoulder. She cringed and Oliver snuggled closer.

"It's okay," she encouraged, trying to smile.

"Marcus is going to be with us." Oliver said it with satisfaction, as if Marcus Palermo solved all of their problems.

The way she looked at it, Marcus was just another problem. He was too handsome. He was too much of a loner. He didn't need or want anyone in his life. And the little boy sitting next to her wanted and needed a father. He would have to be told the truth, and when that happened, she knew he would want to stay with Marcus.

"I know he is going to be there." She bit down on her lip as they hit a few potholes. The first responder had warned her that a ride with Doc Parker could be worse than the accident. She now understood the warning.

The car stopped at what appeared to be an abandoned convenience store. "What is this?"

Doc had already gotten out and was opening the door to help her. "My office."

"Oh."

"Don't worry, it's better than it looks. I know, an RN like yourself, you're used to city clinics and hospitals. This serves us just fine."

"I'm sure it does." She eased herself out of the car and waited for Oliver. He had been so brave, but he now had big tears in his eyes. One broke loose and slid down his cheek. He swiped it away and managed a fierce look.

"Are you okay, sweetheart?" She leaned close to the little boy.

He nodded and sniffed away the tears. "I'm good. I'm going to be a bull rider someday. Like Marcus. So I have to be tough."

She wanted to sigh at that revelation. Oliver

needed male role models. That was all. He was attaching himself to Marcus not because of the connection but because he represented everything a kid like Oliver wanted. Marcus was tough. He had lived an exciting life. He was a world champion. Of course Oliver wanted to be like him.

Doc cleared his throat as he looked from her to the little boy. "We'd best get you inside and put that shoulder back in the socket. Marcus will be here any minute. He just had a hard time keeping up with me." The last was said with a grin and, she thought, a bit of misplaced pride.

He led them through a dismally decorated waiting room to a small exam room. Lissa gave Oliver what she hoped to be a reassuring look.

"Oliver, do you want to sit out in the waiting room? I bet Dr. Parker has a book you can look at."

Doc rubbed a hand through thinning gray hair. "Books. Yes, I should have books. I keep meaning to get more. I have young ones that come in and books are something they love to take home with them. I can't deny a child a book. And it's Doc, not Dr. Parker."

He walked away mumbling about books and toys and a shopping list. Oliver followed him out of the exam room, leaving Lissa alone. She closed her eyes and said a quick prayer. For her shoulder. For the doctor. And for the situation with Marcus and Oliver.

Her peace was short-lived. She heard male voices from the waiting room. Doc's more gentle voice resonated through the door. She couldn't make out his words. There were footsteps in the hall, a door closed, more talking. She heard Oliver telling them about how hard he hit his head and that he was sure he must have a headache. She smiled at his matter-of-fact assessment of his condition. He was fine, she assured herself. He wouldn't be talking and laughing if he wasn't okay.

And then the door opened and Marcus Palermo charged through, looking ragged and worn. Without greeting her, he took off his hat and hung it on a hook. He brushed a hand through curly, dark hair and then he seemed to remember her presence.

"What happened?"

"I'm fine, thank you. So is Oliver." She didn't have the patience for overbearing, take-charge men.

"I'm sorry—" he shook his head "—I shouldn't have let you leave in this weather."

"You didn't have a choice. I'm an adult and I made the decision." She grimaced as a hot flash of pain hit her shoulder, payment for what should have been a carefree shrug.

"It wasn't safe," he said as he took a seat on the rolling stool next to the exam table.

"I'm twenty-eight. I know how to drive in the rain. Could you please go sit with Oliver? He's alone. I don't want him to be alone." She also didn't want to be told what she could or couldn't do. Her short relationship with Troy Larson had taught her that there was a fine line between a caring man who wanted to spend time with a woman and a controlling jerk who didn't trust her out of his sight.

"Oliver isn't alone. He's with Doc and my brother, Alex." He pinned her with his dark gaze. "Doc said your shoulder is dislocated."

"Yes. It's happened before and it isn't too bad this time. I'm more worried about Oliver. If you could sit with him. Make sure he isn't nauseated. Watch that his speech doesn't slur."

The door opened and Doc stepped inside the cramped room with the green carpet and mustard-yellow walls. He glanced at his watch and then at her.

"Well, young lady, let's get this shoulder taken care of so we don't miss lunch. Essie has the best enchiladas on Tuesdays."

She nodded toward the door. "Cowboy, you should go. This isn't going to be pleasant."

Doc cackled at her warning. "You think I haven't reset a bone or two for these boys? Marcus could probably set this shoulder with his eyes closed. He only lets me do it because he's polite. Shy, quiet type, you know."

She closed her eyes and nodded. "Yes, he is quiet."

"Well, I can't fix everything," Doc said softly. She wondered what he meant by that. "Now, let me see."

He felt her shoulder and then gently rotated her arm. She took a deep breath, knowing what would come next. Still, she wasn't prepared. Not for the bolt of lightning-deep pain or the arm that encircled her, holding her steady. Marcus smelled of rain, soap and aftershave, the kind of spicy scent that made a girl think of mountains and lakes. For a brief moment it took her mind off the pain in her shoulder. He was strong. Definitely the kind of guy a girl could lean on. But just for a moment.

Doc handed her a couple of pills and a glass of water. "I'm sorry about that. No way to do it without causing a lot of hurt. I'm going to put some ice on your shoulder and we'll put that arm in a sling. I guess you'll know when it's time to start exercising it a bit. And I guess I don't have to tell you not to drive. From the looks of your car, it won't be going anywhere for a while."

She briefly closed her eyes. "I need to call my insurance. I can get a rental."

"That won't be possible." Marcus gave her a sympathetic look. Maybe a grimace. She wasn't sure. "Not only is your car totaled but the bridge is going to be under water."

"I'm not sure what to do," she admitted as the full impact of the situation hit home.

"For now you stay put." Marcus's voice, soft and raspy, had an edge to it. And she got it. He wasn't any happier about this than she was. He probably thought he'd seen the last of her.

Doc cleared his throat. "If I might be so bold, Essie is in the waiting room. She heard about the accident on the scanner and she came right over. She's a bit nosy. But she's ready to take you to her place."

"Doc, could we have a minute alone?" Marcus asked.

"You and me?" Doc didn't show a hint of amusement, but a knowing twinkle lit his eyes.

"Doc," Marcus's tone held a warning.

Lissa cringed. Controlling men. They were all the same. When he'd dated Sammy, had he asked her where she was going? Who she was going with? When she would call him?

Doc looked from one to the other of them

and sighed. "Right, I'll go check on that young man of yours."

Lissa watched Doc slip through the door, closing it tightly behind him. Marcus pinched the bridge of his nose.

"Stay with Aunt Essie," he said finally. "The flooding is going to be worse. The next few days could get pretty bad. You obviously can't drive with your right arm in a sling."

Stay. She knew that this was the fork in the road. There were many in life, and this time the choice was hers and it would affect not only her life but Oliver's. And Marcus's.

"Fine, I'll stay. But I have conditions."

"Name your price."

She shook her head at the reference to money. "There is no price. I'm not after money. I'm after your time, Marcus. While we are here, you have to spend time with Oliver. And at some point we have to tell him that you're his father."

"I don't know how to be a father."

Of course he didn't. But what man did? It happened to everyone. People decided to have children. They became parents. It wasn't as if they knew how to do it beforehand. It was on-the-job training.

"Maybe you don't know how, but you'll learn. I'll be here and I can help."

A muscle ticked in his jaw. "That's a lot to put on a man who, until you showed up, hadn't planned on having a family. Ever."

"I understand. But you do have a son. He's sitting in that waiting room and he thinks you're the best thing ever."

"He's a good kid," Marcus said softly in his gruff way. She realized now it wasn't that he was gruff. It was his voice.

"Yes, he is."

She sighed, knowing the decision she had to make, and knowing that it meant eventually losing Oliver to this man, his father. "I have vacation time," she told him. "I'll give you three weeks to get this figured out. And I'll help you as much as I can. But I don't want to lose Oliver, either." And she hoped that in the end she wouldn't lose him, not completely.

"I understand."

Her heart pounded hard against her ribs as she realized she'd just given this man a piece of her life. She'd given him a part of her heart. The part that belonged to a little boy.

As she tried to process her emotions, he took her hand gently in his and held it briefly, before shaking it to seal the deal.

That gentleness undid some of her fears and multiplied others. She'd come to Bluebonnet Springs thinking it would be easy to discount him as a parent. He would be the angry, difficult man that Sammy had described, and Lissa would have walked away with Oliver, thinking she had done her best.

But he wasn't that man. If the eyes were the mirror of the soul, then he wasn't cruel and unfeeling. He wasn't a monster. He had been wounded. Deeply. And he cared for his family. Very much.

Chapter Four

The rain continued to come down, and by Thursday, as Marcus made his way up the long gravel drive to Essie's house, it looked as if the ponds had turned to lakes and the ditches were streams carrying debris all the way to the main road. They were in trouble. They all knew it. Farmers were moving cattle away from the spring that ran through town and the countryside. Roads were being closed left and right.

The rain they'd had since Monday was mild compared to what was coming over the weekend.

The house came into view, a two-story ranch house with large windows, a lot of stucco and wood trim, and warmth. Essie's house always felt like home. The Palermo kids had all done their share of running to Essie's. And then Jesse had dragged them home. Essie, like most people around town, hadn't liked to cross her nephew. For the most part she had avoided him.

He parked beneath the portico at the side of the house and got out. The sky was heavy with clouds and the air was thick with humidity. He hurried up the steps to the side door that led through the breakfast sunroom to the kitchen. Essie smiled a greeting and went back to making coffee.

"I closed the café. People don't need to be driving to town in this, not for my biscuits and gravy." She explained her presence without looking up from the coffeemaker.

"They'd drive through a blizzard for your biscuits and gravy," he assured her as he gave her a quick hug. "How are your guests?"

"Sleeping. Lissa had a restless night and finally slept in the recliner. I have a casserole in the oven and cinnamon rolls are ready to eat. Which do you want?"

"Both," he told her as he grabbed a plate and snatched one of the rolls. "But I'll start with this."

"I'm sure you've already had a full day."

"Been up since five this morning. Fed, moved cattle, loaded up my horses and took them to Alex's place." By Alex's place he meant the Palermo ranch. But he was content to let it be Alex and Marissa's home.

"It's only going to get worse," Essie told him as she poured two cups of coffee. "Have you seen the radar?"

"Yeah, and thanks for the optimism. I thought you would be praying for it to stop."

"I'm praying, but sometimes it rains and the only thing you can do is have the buckets ready. I told Lissa they're welcome to stay here as long as they need."

"Thank you."

She gave him a look over the rim of her coffee cup, her dark eyes saying more than words. She was wanting to know how he could have walked away from a child.

"I didn't know," he defended. "Do you think I would have left a kid on his own if I'd known?"

"I would hope not. But what you did isn't as important as what you do going forward."

"I know that. I'm a different person." A completely different person. He was a new man with new faith. That didn't make him whole, but he could at least look at the situation with those new eyes.

The only person he couldn't make it right with was Sammy. Because she was gone. The thought settled like a heavy weight in his chest.

They'd both been too damaged to make a relationship work, but he should have done better by her. He should have called.

He guessed this was a real lesson in thinking things through and knowing there would always be consequences. And the consequence appeared, sleepy-eyed and dark hair tousled. He had a thumb jammed in his mouth and he wore red plaid pajamas that were a little too big on him.

"Good morning, Oliver." Aunt Essie swooped his son up and hugged him tight. "Are you hungry?"

It was a shame Essie had never had kids of her own. Instead, she mothered everyone she came into contact with. Including Bea, her cook and chief problem maker at the café.

Oliver nodded as an answer to Essie's question and pulled the thumb from his mouth. He let his dark gaze settle on Marcus. He was waiting.

Marcus cleared his throat. "Morning, Oliver. How about coffee?"

Essie rolled her eyes. "He's five, Marcus. He drinks milk."

Marcus winked at his son. "I knew that, but I like to get Essie all riled up. I'll pour you some milk and get you a cinnamon roll."

Marcus pulled milk out of the fridge and got a glass.

"I like chocolate milk," Oliver informed them.

"I think I have cocoa." Essie went to the cabinet. "I'll measure it into the milk and you can stir."

Oliver nodded and stuck to Essie's side as she produced the container of chocolate powder, and Marcus set the glass of milk on the counter. He leaned a hip against the counter and watched.

They were stirring the milk when Lissa appeared. He glanced her way and quickly averted his gaze. She was bleary-eyed with her dark hair going in all directions. She might not have slept a lot, but he guessed she'd slept hard. She noticed his amusement and frowned.

"You're not allowed to laugh at me. It isn't like I can untangle this mess." She lifted her left hand to try to smooth the strands that framed her face.

"You look fine," he said. As far as lines went, or compliments, that probably rated bottom of the scale.

Behind him, Essie chuckled. He shot her a look as she pulled the casserole from the oven.

Lissa glared at him as she continued to brush her fingers through her hair. He reached out, smoothing the silky strands of hair, letting them slide through his fingers. It was about the worst thing he could have done, making that connection with her, touching her. He'd meant to help. Instead, he stood there all tangled up in something he hadn't expected. Her breath caught as he slid his fingers free of the strands of hair. Blue eyes caught and held his attention.

Behind him the pan banged on the counter with meaning. He stepped back. "It looks fine. I can braid it for you, if that would make it easier."

"No." She shook her head. "I'll leave it down."

"Did you manage to get any sleep?" he asked.

"Some… Enough. But the shoulder does feel a bit better today." She cleared her throat. "That casserole smells so good."

"It's ready," Essie piped up. There was a smirk this time when she made eye contact with Marcus. He didn't like this version of his aunt. She usually minded her own business. Now it felt as if she had a plan, a plot, and he was the victim.

He needed something else to focus on. That would be Oliver. The little boy looked kind of lost. Marcus ruffled his hair.

"Want to help me set the table, little man?"

Oliver nodded and followed him the way

Lucky the dog sometimes did. As if he was just waiting for something good. A pat on the head, a bone. Marcus knew that this boy, his son, wanted and needed more from him.

He pulled plates from the cabinet and silverware from the drawer. He handed the forks and knives to Oliver.

"Can you take those to the breakfast room?"

Marcus led Oliver to the sun-filled breakfast room. It might mean losing his man card, but he loved the room with the white trim and pale yellow walls. Ferns hung from hooks in the ceiling, and potted plants filled the corners. The window seat, cushioned with aqua-and-yellow pillows, looked out over the field. Essie's cat, Midas, stretched and graced Marcus with a contented feline look.

Essie had placed the casserole on a trivet in the center of the round table. Marcus sat down opposite Lissa and then realized that more was required from him. Oliver stared at the casserole with big eyes and anticipation. Essie had gone back to the kitchen for napkins, so Marcus took over serving.

Oliver's eyes widened at the portion of casserole and the cinnamon roll with icing that Marcus piled on his plate.

As the boy dug in, Marcus was amazed and a bit lost. He'd missed out. He'd missed five years' worth of breakfasts. Five birthdays. Five Christmases. Walking. Talking. Every single thing that would have meant building a relationship, precious moments stolen from them both.

Two days ago he had been in denial. Today he got swept up in the anger and unfairness of it. It didn't matter that he believed his son would be better off without him. What mattered was that he was the dad and he should have known his son. He wanted to blame the woman sitting across from him, but it hadn't been up to her. And as mad as he was about the situation, he understood why Sammy had blocked him from Oliver's life.

A hand touched his arm. He glanced down at the woman seated next to Oliver. Her eyes were warm and met his with compassion. She gave his arm a squeeze, transferring that compassion with her touch. He shook his head, clearing his thoughts.

Without asking, he served her a portion of the casserole. And then he grabbed his coffee and left. Because he couldn't look at Oliver without feeling guilt. Without feeling angry.

He walked through the house to the covered front porch, where he stood sipping his coffee, trying to get his better self back. The door behind him opened. He expected Essie.

Instead, Lissa stepped out to join him. She was the last person he'd expected to come chasing after him. She was probably the last person he *wanted* chasing after him. For any reason. She made him question himself a little too much. She made him want things he had told himself he didn't want.

He'd spent a lifetime building himself up as a happy bachelor. Okay, maybe not happy. A bachelor. Single. Living for himself. No worries about hurting people or letting them down. He didn't want or need a woman in his life.

At least that was what he'd been telling himself for a long time.

"You should go eat," he said, once again staring out over the rain-soaked farm.

"So should you. And yet you're out here fighting with the past and someone who isn't here to argue back." She stood next to him now. Man, she smelled good. Like sunshine.

"Yeah, well, I do like to argue. And I have every right to be angry."

"You do." She agreed, and that surprised him. "When Sammy found out she was pregnant, I told her to call you, to give you a chance. She said she couldn't do it…that she'd had a lifetime of men with commitment-phobia and she wasn't going to have you in her life just to have you walk out on them."

"I wouldn't have walked out."

She shrugged. "Maybe not."

"What made you decide to find me now, after all this time?" He glanced down at her. She was only a few inches shorter than he was, which made it easy to look her in the eye, easy to see her distrust.

"I don't know. I love Oliver and I don't want to lose him. But it was never right to keep him from you."

"I missed out on five years. He doesn't even know me. I'm a bull rider you decided to visit one day. He has to wonder why."

"I'm sure he does. And we'll tell him."

"When?"

"Soon." She moved away from him. "Have you read the letter?"

"No, I haven't."

"You should."

Yeah, he guessed he should. He had it in his pocket, a crumpled piece of paper with a lawyer's signature on the bottom.

He skimmed the letter, wishing he had read it sooner, read it somewhere private. Instead, the words jumped out at him as Lissa stood by the door to Essie's, her expression concerned and distrustful, all at the same time.

Sammy hadn't trusted him to be a father. She had given Lissa custody and the power to decide if he was capable of parenting his son. He raised his head, making eye contact with the woman who held his future in her hands. A woman who clearly didn't like him any more than Sammy had.

"I guess I can fight you. It would take a DNA test and not much else." He wasn't even sure why he uttered those words. He hadn't planned to keep Oliver. He knew the boy was better off with Lissa.

But he'd been considered unfit. And that made him mad. It made him want to fight.

"Yeah, I guess you could." She stood a little taller, and he guessed she was trying not to show her fear.

He shoved the letter back into his pocket. "This should never have happened. It shouldn't be you here giving me ultimatums. It shouldn't be me trying to figure out which end is up."

"I know that. But we can't go back and undo what Sammy did. We can only figure out what is best going forward."

"I guess so. But I wish I knew what it was you wanted from me. What kind of hoops do I have to jump through to earn your approval?"

"Come back inside, have breakfast with your son. Be a dad."

Be a dad. He'd met men who were fathers, real fathers. He'd watched them with their sons, encouraging them, disciplining without anger. They were men he looked up to. And the type of man he'd never considered becoming. Until now, when Sammy had ultimately put the ball in his court. And a son in his life. He followed Lissa inside and found himself wishing he wasn't a scarred-up, angry Palermo. If he wasn't, he might have tried to come up with a response that made her smile, something better than "Fine."

After the breakfast dishes were cleared, Lissa made a phone call to her foster parents. She'd called them on Tuesday, but she'd promised to keep in touch.

"How are you doing?" Jane asked, her voice bringing a sheen of moisture to Lissa's eyes. She quickly blinked it away.

"I'm good. I'm taking your advice and staying. I know you all could come get me. And I'll have a rental car as soon as I can get somewhere and find one. But you were right. For Oliver's sake, I need to see this through."

"Do you feel more optimistic about his father?"

The question brought the conversation to a standstill. *More optimistic* probably wasn't the way she'd put it. She was dangerously attracted to him and yet she knew better. Her last relationship had been a disaster. Troy had been a dysfunctional disaster, the product of a son raised by a controlling father. It felt like a repeat, even if Marcus wasn't anything like Troy. If anything, he was surprisingly gentle. It didn't make sense that this was the man Sammy had walked away from and refused to tell he had a son.

She wished she'd questioned her foster sister a little more, asking questions about why the relationship had ended. She wished she'd pushed for answers. Something more than two dysfunctionals don't make a positive.

No, she had to keep her thoughts focused on what was best for Oliver. She had to make the right choices for the little boy.

She told her foster mom that same thing. "It isn't that I'm optimistic. I just see that there might have been two sides to Sammy's story. And I want to do the right thing for Oliver."

"And you don't want to lose our little man in the process."

That part hurt the most. "Exactly."

The call ended and she stood on the covered front porch, watching as rain poured down in seemingly limitless amounts. The gray sky didn't show any signs of blue. The clouds were heavy and hung low. Fog rolled over the distant hills.

It was quiet here. The kind of quiet that made a person feel as if they were alone on the planet. She might have felt peace if she hadn't been worried about what the future held for herself and for Oliver. It wasn't as if she'd lit out for Bluebonnet Springs with no thought toward the future, no prayers for guidance. But now everything felt different. Marcus wasn't who she'd thought he would be. In Bluebonnet Springs, Oliver had family. Aunts, uncles and cousins. She didn't know what she'd expected to find here, but it wasn't this family looking out for each other.

The door opened behind her. She wasn't surprised that it was Marcus. He eyed her suspiciously. It seemed this was going to be their relationship, circling each other, questioning, worrying.

"Everything okay?" he asked as he moved to her side.

"Yes. I just wanted to touch base with my family. I wanted to let them know I'm staying so we can work this out."

"You think a few weeks will fix this situation?"

"I'm an optimist." Or at least trying to be one.

He half grinned at her words, and the faint

sign of amusement caught her by surprise. "Yeah, me too."

She laughed. "Right."

"I even think this rain will let up a bit and maybe we won't have to build an ark to get out of Texas."

"I hope you're right about that."

He had a cowboy hat in his hand and he placed it on his head, adjusting it a little. His slightly long hair curled out from under, making him appear younger, less hard around the edges.

"I have to run over to my place to check on my livestock, and then I'll swing by my brother's place to assess things there. Oliver is curled up on the sofa watching a cartoon."

"Is that an invitation for me to go with you?" She regretted the words the moment they left her mouth.

He pushed the hat back a bit and gave her a long look.

"I don't have to go," she said.

"You can go. But fair warning…it might not be fun and you'll definitely get wet. Might want to see if Essie has a raincoat you can use."

She nodded and slipped into the house to see what she could find. Maybe she'd find her common sense. Essie seemed to have plenty of that. She might lend some, in case Lissa's had taken a long leave of absence.

Essie did have a raincoat. When Lissa stepped back outside, Marcus had disappeared. She heard a truck start and waited on the front porch as he drove to pick her up.

She stepped off the porch expecting to race across the lawn to the vehicle. Instead, he pulled close and jumped out to open the door for her.

"You didn't have to do that," she told him as she climbed in.

In response, he closed the door and hurried back to the driver's side. "I do have some manners."

"I know you do." She met his gaze. "Let's try to be friends."

"I'm trying," he told her in his low, gruff voice. "You have to give a guy a few days to figure things out and get over feeling like he's had his legs kicked out from under him."

"I know." She pulled her seat belt around and he reached over to click it into place for her. "Thank you."

"I'm not going to take him from you," he said as they headed down the long driveway back to the main road.

The sting of tears took her by surprise. She

wiped at them, and when he handed her a handkerchief, she shook her head.

"I'm fine."

"Yeah, of course you are." He shoved the handkerchief into her hand. "I know he needs you. I know he doesn't need a scarred-up, dysfunctional cowboy for a dad."

"I think you're wrong," she said, and the words took her by surprise. It was more than a platitude; it was the truth.

"I'm not wrong." He pulled onto the road. "I know myself better than anyone. I want him to know that I'm his dad. I want to spend time with him. But he needs you in his life."

"I think he might need us both. As the adults in his life, we have to find the best way to give him stability."

There was silence except for tires humming on wet pavement. Lissa studied the strong profile of the man sitting next to her. She couldn't see the left side of his face, but she wondered about the scar on his cheek. He glanced her way, caught her staring.

"Was the scar from bull riding?" she asked.

"It's a gift from my father," he said simply and kept driving.

"What?"

"The scar on my face. My father did that. I've always heard that the fruit doesn't fall far from the vine. If that's the case, I'm his son and I can't outrun the fact that his DNA is in me. I'm not going to subject another kid to the life we led when he was alive."

Lissa's heart constricted. It made her sad that he believed that about himself, that he would be a father like his own. But what could she tell him? She didn't know him well enough to reassure him otherwise.

She thought of another old saying and she smiled. "The proof is in the pudding."

"What?" He gave her a quick glance and then returned his focus to the road, steering around water that covered their lane.

"I don't know what it means. But if you want to throw out old sayings, I thought I'd toss out one of my own."

He grimaced and made a grunting noise that might have been a chuckle. "I think the point of a saying is that it should fit the situation. My dad was evil," he told her. "He wasn't a good person. I'm his son. The fruit doesn't fall far from the vine."

"But the proof is in the pudding," she repeated. "I don't know what proof is in the pudding, but I'm saying we should look at who you are and how you really treat those around you instead of insinuating you're evil just because your father was."

"That's real nice of you to think that." He hit his blinker and a moment later turned onto the back road that led to his place. "But I'm sure Sammy filled you in on exactly the kind of person I am. If you thought differently, you would have found me a little sooner. Sammy would have called me the day she found out she was pregnant. So there's the proof that is in the pudding."

"So Oliver is destined to be a horrible person, a terrible man and a bad father because your dad was a terrible person?"

He grinned at that. "Oh, good one. I think you get the point for this set. No, he isn't destined to be bad. He had Sammy and he has you. You'll make sure he grows up to be a decent person."

At one point Lissa could have left town, taken Oliver, and that would have been the end of it. But she had stayed and now their lives seemed to be intertwined. And the nurse in her, the person who cared and wanted to fix others, wouldn't let her walk away.

She knew better than to take Marcus on as a project. She knew one or both, maybe all three of them, would be hurt in the process.

But she was committed. She had a few weeks to show him he could be a decent father, that he wasn't destined to be his father's son any more than Oliver was. If they believed in redemption, and she knew they both did, then they had to believe hearts could change and the past didn't have to control the future.

Rather than finding reasons he couldn't have Oliver, she would help him to discover the reasons he *could*.

It seemed like the perfect plan as long as she could keep her own heart intact in the process. Marcus might be rough around the edges, but he was also chivalrous and kind. And when he smiled, she forgot that a relationship with a broken man was the last thing she wanted.

Chapter Five

From his parking spot next to the house, Marcus could see the normally lazy creek already out of its banks. With the rain still coming down, it would only get higher. He got out of the truck and Lissa joined him, standing so close that for a moment he was distracted by her. And that couldn't happen.

He needed to move his tractor and ATV to higher ground. The barn sat on a slight rise, and he didn't think water would get in there.

"Wow, there's a lot of power in that water." Lissa whistled low as they walked toward the creek.

"Yeah, enough to tear down a building or move a vehicle."

"Will it rise up to your house?"

He glanced back at the hundred-year-old

home. "I guess it's probably gotten up there more than once. But that old house is solid."

He got lost for a minute, thinking of the Brown family who had lived there for nearly a century. Passed down from generation to generation, they'd built onto this house as the family grew. The house had history. A good history. He guessed that was what he liked about the place. It was rambling, ancient, but folks had been happy here. He couldn't imagine losing it this way.

"You okay?" she asked, her voice soft.

"Yeah, I'm good. Just thinking about that house. I'd hate for anything to happen to it."

"It means a lot to you, this house? Has it always been in your family?"

This was why he avoided conversation. People wanted to dig into his past, figure him out. Women were especially bad about digging. The scar. His voice. Those things attracted women who liked fixer-uppers.

He didn't need fixing.

But she was giving him that intent, questioning look, so he would give her the story she wanted.

"The house and property belonged to the Browns. When I was a kid, I used to walk down here, escaping my house and my dad. Mattie Brown made the best peanut butter cookies. And tea. She used to make me some kind of herbal tea. I don't know what she put in it, but it helped…"

He caught himself and shook his head. She didn't need that much information about his life. "I enjoyed visiting. They were a decent family. They liked each other. When it came up for sale, after all the kids moved away, I decided it shouldn't go to a stranger."

She was walking toward the back of his house, and he followed. The rain started to come down in sheets again and thunder rumbled in the distance. A second later the two of them were running. He reached the back door first and opened it for her. They stepped inside, dripping wet. It was a small space and they were face-to-face, both with water dripping. She swiped at her face with her hand, and then she touched his face, her hand brushing across the scar that he'd prefer most people didn't notice.

He stilled beneath her hesitant touch and she withdrew her hand. He grabbed a towel off the shelf over the washer and handed it to her.

"Liked each other?" she asked as she handed him the towel.

He blinked, confused.

"The people who lived here?" she clarified.

"I guess families should like each other, shouldn't they?"

In all the years he'd known Mattie and George Brown, he'd never seen them raise a hand to a person or an animal. George had worked with Marcus, teaching him to train horses. He hadn't realized back then that George was teaching him patience. Old and a little hard of hearing, George had taught Marcus to trust. There had been few people in his life whom he'd given that trust to.

The one person he still didn't trust, not completely, was himself. He didn't trust himself to not be like his own father.

"I had a neighbor." Lissa's voice broke into his thoughts, bringing him back to the present. "I called her *Tía* Theresa. She wasn't my aunt, but she would have been a wonderful aunt. She lived in the apartment next to ours. When things got rough in our apartment, I would sit in the stairwell. Theresa would join me on the steps, bringing me cookies or food." Lissa took a breath, then went on. "She told me about her husband—he'd been a police officer. He'd always treated her right, she said. Never laid a hand on her. Some men are like that, she would tell me. Some men don't hurt their women or their daughters. Not that the men my mother had in our apartment were husband or father. They were just the men she brought home."

The words she'd spoken hung between them. He didn't have to ask. He knew she'd been hurt.

"She hot-lined my mother," she said after a while. "She's the reason the state took me into custody and I went to live with the Simms family. Sammy and I were foster children together. It changed our lives. Because of the Simms, we had a family. I still have them."

He stood up, uncomfortable with the stories they were sharing and needing to shake off whatever it was about her that rattled him. He shook his head at that. He wasn't a liar, not even to himself. What it was about her was possibly everything. From her smile to the soft way she spoke and then her story. It connected them in a way he hadn't expected.

Or wanted.

The only way to sever the connection was to send her and his son packing and never see them again. That had seemed like a good idea, until it hadn't. As much as he didn't trust himself to be the man anyone would count on, he also didn't want to be the dad who walked out on his son.

He'd learned a long time ago that some things took hard work, and it appeared that parenting would be added to that list. He might not have learned the art of parenting from his own mother and father, but that didn't mean he had an excuse for not trying.

"I need to start moving equipment before that creek comes up any farther." He pulled a jacket off the hook by the door.

He thought she'd stay put. Instead, she grabbed the rain jacket she'd borrowed from Essie.

"I'll help."

Of course she would.

He gave her a long look, shook his head and walked out the door. He walked fast, letting her hurry to catch up with him.

She laughed, the sound light and a little breathless. "Oh, wow, you're running because we shared our stories and that let me in a little too close for comfort, didn't it? Emotion is your Kryptonite. You're better with the surface stuff. A smile, a joke, a teasing look, maybe dinner."

"I don't do one-night stands, if that's what you're insinuating." He checked back to see if she was keeping up. "I don't do relationships. Period. I haven't dated since Sammy."

As the information slipped out, he rubbed a hand over his face and groaned.

"Really?" Now her tone was wistful, as if she'd just learned the one great truth.

"Really," he bit out. "Now, if you don't mind, I have work to do."

"Why?" she prodded, and he knew what she meant.

"Because it's raining, and if I don't move some equipment, it could get flooded."

"Dating."

"Yeah, I knew what you meant. I just hoped I could sidetrack you. And you know why I don't date. I've been working on my life and that meant not dragging someone else into the mess."

"How's that going?"

"You can see for yourself." He hurried under the roof of the equipment shed. She was right there with him.

"Yes, I can see."

She was standing too close and he almost forgot his vow to work on himself and not get tangled up in relationships that always ended with someone getting hurt. He didn't want to hurt her. And he didn't want their relationship to be awkward, not when it might hurt Oliver.

Step one in being a dad meant putting his son first. Ahead of his own crazy, mixed-up emotions. If he kissed her—and he was tempted—that would confuse the issue. It would put his priorities off balance.

Trouble was, he really wanted to kiss her. And she was looking at him like she might want to kiss him back.

The right thing to do here was to put distance between them. Self-sacrifice at its best. "I need to get busy."

"How can I help?" she asked.

She could go back to Essie's. Or even to San Antonio. She grinned at him knowingly, as if she could read his thoughts. That smile was becoming familiar. It showed that she'd survived her childhood and she still found things to laugh about. Still found ways to enjoy life. She enjoyed goading him.

"You could let me get some work done," he grumbled.

"I can't leave. I don't have a car." She patted his chest with the palm of her hand. "Let's get something straight, cowboy. I'm not chasing after you the way the girls did back in your rodeo days. I'm here to help you build a relationship with your son. End of story. The last thing I want is a damaged male with an over-inflated ego."

Of course he was the last thing she would be looking for in a man. The ego she'd talked about took a bit of a hit, but he shrugged it off. Instead of arguing, he climbed into his tractor and leaned down, reaching for her left hand. She took the offer and he pulled her into the cab of the tractor with him. "Don't get any ideas. I'm not letting you drive a piece of equipment that cost me a small fortune."

"I wasn't going to ask." She said it sweetly and he knew she'd been tempted.

As they drove through the field, he used the tractor to pick up a bale of hay.

"How much land do you have?"

"Five hundred acres," he answered.

"That's no small amount." She had been watching the landscape roll past. Now she turned to look at him. "You've done well with bull riding."

"Yeah, I've done well. I made good investments."

"Did you?" She didn't push. Her gaze darted to the rain-soaked fields, the cattle grazing at the top of the hill. "And here I thought you couldn't climb out of the bottle long enough to feed yourself, let alone a couple hundred head of cattle."

"Thanks for the compliment."

"In a way it is. I was wrong about that. You obviously feed your cattle."

"Yes, I feed my cattle. And I haven't been climbing in any bottles. Not for several years."

"Did you ever want to do anything else, other than ride bulls or ranch?"

To her it probably seemed like a logical question. People must have other dreams and ambitions. She didn't know what it meant to grow up with Jesse Palermo controlling a person's every action. As a kid he hadn't dreamed of anything other than escaping.

"Nope, it's always been this for me. I'm dyslexic." The admission slipped out. Not normally what he considered a conversation starter.

"I didn't know that," she responded.

"It isn't as if I tell everyone I meet." Or anyone, really. His siblings knew. Essie knew.

"Are you saying that is why you didn't have other goals?"

"No, it's just a part of who I am. I spent my childhood acting out, getting in trouble and definitely not studying."

It was only lately that he learned he knew about more than livestock. He had a gift with the stock market. He'd invested his earnings and he'd seen a pretty decent return on his investment in the last couple of years.

He didn't know her well enough to trust her with that information. *Trust*. That was something he was working on.

His phone rang, saving him the trouble of

having to answer the questions he knew she would have asked. She was that type of female, the kind that couldn't let anything rest. He would have liked to say that bothered him, but it didn't.

Sitting next to her, he didn't feel much like Marcus Palermo, the brawling bull rider. He felt like someone who ought to be thinking about growing up.

Lissa half listened to the phone call as the tractor bounced across the field. Rain that had let up returned, heavier, bouncing off the windshield of the tractor. Deftly, as if he didn't have to think through the actions, Marcus moved big, round bales of hay. After several minutes he ended the call and turned the tractor back toward the barn. He drove through the open gate and up the drive to park on a hill a distance behind the house.

"I paid too much to have that tractor taken downstream."

"Do you think that will happen?"

"They're expecting a pretty good crest at midnight tonight, and if this rain doesn't stop, it'll get even higher. They're stacking sandbags in front of some stores in town, hoping to keep the water out."

He parked the tractor and reached up for her hand. "Careful, the ground is slick."

She eased down, careful of her now throbbing shoulder. When he gave her a questioning look, she managed a grimace that she hoped resembled a smile.

"Pretty sore?"

"A little," she admitted.

"I have a heating pad inside. While I get some things moved, you can take a break, maybe have a cup of tea that will help."

"Tea that will help?"

"Chamomile." He walked off as he said it and she hurried to catch up, ducking through the door beneath his arm that held it open.

Big tough bull rider, scar down his left cheek and a broken voice, but he drank a tea known for its calming properties. He led her through the kitchen to the living room. The house was another surprise. It was sparsely furnished but cozy. The walls were shades of pale blue and a light gray. The furniture looked as if it belonged in a seaside cottage.

As she wandered, examining the paintings on the walls, he pulled a heating pad from the closet. She accepted it and followed him back to the kitchen to watch as he started a pot of coffee and made a cup of chamomile tea.

His movements were spare, efficient, controlled. Not once did he smile. He needed to smile. Oliver was a funny kid who liked to joke. What if Marcus didn't understand that about his son?

What if Marcus lost his temper? What if he didn't hug Oliver, tuck him in at night or comfort him when he was afraid?

She told herself to stop. She could go through dozens of "what if" questions. She could spend her life worrying. But what good did worry do?

"What happened to your voice?" She asked the question she'd been wondering about since she'd met him.

The microwave dinged. He pulled the cup of tea out, stirred in a spoonful of honey and handed it to her. "Let it steep a few minutes. And my voice is none of your concern."

"Isn't it?"

"Do you think it will affect my ability to be a dad? Is that the reason for all of the questions? Are you scoring me on my emotional state, my parenting, my ability to be an adult?"

"No, of course not."

He gave her a long, steady look devoid of anger. "It isn't something I talk about. Ever."

"I see."

He took the heating pad from her and plugged it in next to the table. "Sit down."

She did as he ordered, sitting with the cup of chamomile tea between her hands, warming her. He adjusted the temperature on the heating pad and settled it on her shoulder. His touch was firm yet gentle. She thought she felt his fingers trace a path across her back. Maybe it was her imagination, that featherlight touch.

She glanced up at him. "I'm not scoring you. And my question wasn't connected to your ability to parent. I genuinely wanted to know. Maybe the nurse in me. Or maybe—" she paused to think through the words she'd planned to say "—as a friend."

"My dad did this," he whispered close to her ear. "And I didn't want to continue the cycle of abuse. I don't want to take a chance that I would leave a child with scars. Oliver is a funny, happy kid. He should stay that way. Every time I get angry I worry that it might be the time I can't control my temper."

And then he walked out the back door, closing it firmly behind him. For the few seconds the door was open, she heard the rain coming down and in the distance the drone of an engine. With the closing door, there was silence once again.

She sat there alone, thinking back to what he'd told her. His father had maimed him, stolen his voice and left him emotionally scarred, as well.

She wanted to go after him, to tell him she was sorry. Sorry he'd been hurt. Sorry she'd pushed him for answers. But she knew when to let a man go. And this one needed to be set free.

Contemplating her next move, she sat there with the tea he'd made her and the heat soaking into her stiff shoulder. As she finished the tea, she realized Marcus didn't know himself very well. He thought a damaged voice, a scarred body and a nightmarish childhood made him a bad person. He'd probably spent a lifetime living up to that reputation, to his past, making sure everyone knew he was damaged goods.

What he failed to see, what she saw, was that he cared. He cared enough about Oliver to turn him over to Lissa. He cared enough about her, a stranger who had shown up on his doorstep with news that had to be shocking, that he would care for her well-being.

As she sat in silent contemplation, the sun came out from behind the clouds. The golden light streamed through the kitchen. And outside she heard a child's laughter. Oliver's laughter.

She unplugged the heating pad and went out the back door in search of Oliver and Marcus. She found them in the front yard. Another man, a carbon copy of Marcus, and yet not, had joined them. Alex Palermo, his twin, had short hair, no jagged scar on his cheek. And he smiled. Truly smiled. He saw her and tipped his hat in a greeting.

A break in the clouds meant the rain had slowed to intermittent sprinkles. She spotted a patch of blue and rays of sunshine streaking across the sky. Maybe the forecast would be wrong and the rain would miss them this time.

"Lissa, did you see the dog?" Oliver hurried to her side, catching hold of her left hand. "He plays dead with his tongue out. And it's funny. You have to watch."

"I'll watch," she promised. "How did you get here?"

"Alex stopped at Aunt Essie's and I wanted to see you and Marcus. She told me if I wore my seat belt I could ride along. But I'm supposed to stay out of the way."

"He isn't staying out of the way," Marcus grumbled, but she saw the tug of his mouth, a hint of a smile.

There was hope for him yet. She'd never been one to give up on a challenge. But the challenge might be in keeping her perspective. She had to turn Marcus Palermo into a father and nothing more.

Chapter Six

Marcus looked at the three people who had invaded his life. And his kitchen. His twin, Alex, had poured himself a cup of coffee and seemed to be settling in for a cozy visit. As if they had time to sit for a cup. If anything, they needed to be on the road, seeing who of their neighbors needed help getting to higher ground.

Oliver had brought Lucky in with them and he made quick work of trying to get the dog to learn to roll over. The dog plodded around, leaving muddy footprints everywhere. Marcus could have told the boy that the dog played dead because it was the easiest trick in the world for an aging hound dog who didn't much care to get off the porch.

Instead of dissuading him, however, he got a box of dog treats out of the cabinet and handed them to his son. "Try this. Sometimes it just takes a treat."

"Hmm," Lissa murmured with meaning.

"Can't teach an old dog new tricks," he told her.

In response she laughed. "With a treat?"

"Probably not." He managed to keep a straight face, but she caught his eye and winked, almost undoing any hold he had on his self-control.

Alex handed him a cup of coffee. "Well, what's the plan?"

He didn't have a plan, other than hitting the road and trying to figure out who needed help and how best to get things done. Those were the thoughts of a man who didn't have a child. He realized that as he stood there with a cup of coffee, watching Oliver play with Lucky. The dog had sprawled out on the floor and occasionally raised a paw in something that resembled shaking.

He looked down at his coffee and wished, for the first time in a long time, that it was something a lot stronger than coffee. As if he knew, Alex poured milk into the cup and gave him a long and meaningful look.

Marcus raised the cup in salute. "Thanks."

"Anytime."

His phone rang. He grabbed it off the counter and walked out the back door. "Pastor?"

"Marcus, any chance you could head your stock trailer to town and load up some belongings? We've got a couple of houses on West Street that are going to be under water by nightfall."

"You got it." He would gladly do something that would keep his mind off whatever other thoughts or temptations were running through his mind. "I'll be there as soon as I can get Oliver and Lissa back to Essie's."

"She's in town at the café, cooking like a madwoman and serving meals to the workers and those who are trying to pack up and get out."

"I'll bring Lissa to help her out. Hopefully, the water won't get up to the café."

"That's our hope. And our prayer." Pastor Matthews spoke as solemnly as Marcus had ever heard. "You're doing okay?"

The question forced him to be honest. "I've been better. I could use a few of those prayers, if you've got some to spare."

"You know I do. Marcus, you can handle this."

"I guess I can handle whatever comes at me."

The sun had gone behind the clouds again

and he headed back inside as more rain began to fall. He caught Lissa in the act of straightening a picture that hung on the wall in the small dining area.

"It's fine, leave it." He looked for his brother and Oliver. Both were missing.

"You did this, didn't you?" She touched the painting of a barn nestled in a field of wildflowers.

"Mighty nosy, aren't you?"

"Curious, not nosy. I'd like to say the painting takes me by surprise, but maybe not. You're not as tough as you'd like everyone to think, cowboy."

"I'm tough enough." He walked off, grabbing his coat from the hook by the door. "We have to go. The water is rising and a few houses will have water in them pretty soon. I'm taking my trailer to empty them out."

"I can help."

He shook his head. "Nope. You're not going to do heavy lifting. And I don't want Oliver there getting hurt. I'll drop you off at Essie's café. She will probably put you to work."

She froze up as he spoke and he stopped, knowing he'd done something wrong. "What?"

"That's very nice of you to want to keep us safe, but I prefer when men discuss things with me rather than giving me orders."

He scratched his thumb along his chin and nodded. "I apologize."

Her expression softened. "No, I'm sorry. I do understand why this is the best plan. We all have our pasts and it's just…" She shrugged.

"Don't apologize," he assured her. "I get it. And if you seriously want to be out in the rain loading furniture into the back of a stock trailer…"

He gave her shoulder a meaningful look.

She grinned. "No, I don't. Let me get Oliver."

"I'm going to hook the trailer to my truck." He nearly bumped into Alex on his way out the back door.

"Where's the fire?" Alex asked, following him to his truck.

"No fire, just a flood. Pastor Matthews asked me to bring my trailer to West Street."

Alex pulled keys out of his pocket. "I'll head home and get mine. What about Oliver and Lissa?"

"I'll drop them at the café."

"Essie's cooking like a madwoman, I imagine. I'd guess Lucy and Marissa are with her."

Marcus shot his brother a look and wasn't surprised to see that gooey love-struck expression on his face when he mentioned his wife. He wasn't surprised that Alex had fallen, maybe surprised it had happened so quickly. They were different people, he and Alex. Twins but nothing alike.

A few minutes later he backed his truck up to the stock trailer, watching in the mirrors to get it lined up and close to the hitch in the bed of the truck. He jumped out, slipping in the mud as rain poured down. Wouldn't it be nice if they could have a break just long enough that they didn't have to do all of this in a downpour? But then, if that happened, they might not have to worry about a flood. Period.

After hooking the trailer to the truck, he turned to find Oliver and Lissa were there. They'd located an umbrella and were huddling together.

"Get in the truck." He opened the door and motioned them inside. "This rain is crazy. The two of you don't need to be out in it."

"I wonder if this is how Noah felt?" Oliver asked as he buckled up in the back of the truck.

Marcus grinned at the serious look on his son's face. Son. That was still going to take some time to get used to. And it made earlier temptations, old temptations, seem like the worst decisions ever. A few years ago he wouldn't have been a candidate for fatherhood. Not in the condition he had been in.

The last thing this kid needed was a dad who

climbed back in the bottle every time he felt a little bit stressed.

Fortunately he had put that life behind him.

If he was going to be a dad, he'd have to find a quick route to being the kind that Oliver deserved. He'd have to be a dad his son could trust. He just wasn't certain how a man went from being footloose to tied down and dependable.

"I'm not sure about this," he mumbled to himself more than to the woman sitting next to him.

She sighed. A quick look in the back seat and he knew why she wasn't responding. Rule number two, don't discuss stressful things in front of children. He had a lot to learn about parenting.

And from the tense woman sitting next to him, he had a lot to learn about Lissa Hart. He wanted her stories. What made her bristle when she thought someone was taking control? It should have bothered him more that she'd managed to get under his skin in such a short amount of time. Surprisingly, it didn't.

Marcus let them out at Essie's café. Lissa hurried up the steps of the café and through the front door with Oliver squeezing in ahead of her. The bell chimed at their entrance. Before she could think, Oliver was hurrying through the not-so-crowded diner in search of the woman who really was his aunt.

Sooner or later, preferably sooner, they'd have to tell him. For now, Essie was a sweet lady who had taken them in and given him permission to call her aunt, and she made yummy food.

Lissa pulled off the raincoat, mindful of her shoulder. Oliver had disappeared into the kitchen. She was alone and she could take a breath and figure out her next move. She shouldn't have let it bother her, that Marcus wanted to tell her the plan. It had felt like taking over. She knew it had been more about what worked best.

It all went back to a childhood where she'd never felt in control of her situation. Life before Jane and Tom Simms had meant never knowing what would happen next. She'd wondered who she would come home to, what her mother's mood would be and how she would get through a night without someone knocking on her door.

She wanted more for herself. She wanted more for Oliver. She wished he had better memories of his mother. Because Sammy had started to spiral out of control after she had her son. She had been clean and sober for years, and then something had happened.

At the back of Lissa's mind she had always wondered if that something had been Marcus Palermo.

"Lissa, good morning. Oliver told us you were out here." Marissa Palermo, Alex's wife, smiled a greeting, but the smile dissolved. "Are you okay?"

"Of course." She managed what she hoped was a cheerful expression. "I'm here to help."

Marissa locked arms with her and they headed for the kitchen. "We can always use help. Essie is making chicken and noodles and she's going to open in an hour. She wants potatoes mashed and biscuits cooked. I hope you're up for a long day."

"With plenty of coffee, I can handle it."

For the next hour they worked hard. Even Oliver pitched in to help. He was the potato masher and Essie told him he mashed those potatoes even better than Bea Maxwell, the cook who seemed to have a penchant for saying whatever came to her mind.

"You're just saying that because he looks like the twins," Bea grumbled. "And they always were your favorites."

"I take exception to that," Lucy Palermo

Scott called out to Bea as she put the finishing touches on the pies they would serve for dessert.

"Watch yourself, Bea." Essie hugged Bea. "We need to focus on cooking."

"I know, I know." Bea waddled off to the sink. "I hope I can wash my hands without getting in trouble."

Lissa sneaked a peek at Oliver. He didn't seem to be listening at all. He was busy mashing potatoes and eating pudding off the spoon Marissa had placed in front of his mouth. The moment cemented for her that this was a family. They were laughing, loving one another and teasing in a fun way. They weren't at all what she'd expected from the offspring of cult leader Jesse Palermo.

His control over his church had been legendary. He'd been a world-famous bull rider, a minister of his own brand of the gospel and a father. What had been hidden had been the abuse of his family. But they'd survived. She could see that in this group of women. They were all survivors.

"Let's get this on the buffet." Essie called out the order and the women started to move, including a few from the community who had come in to help.

Lucy moved to Lissa's side as the women worked to get food to the warming trays. Oliver was given serving spoons to carry out. Lissa was very aware that Lucy had something to say. It was obvious in the way she watched the others leave.

"Do you plan on taking him back to San Antonio?" Lucy finally asked. "If he's my nephew, I want to know him. And he deserves to be here with his father, with aunts and uncles and cousins."

Lissa blanched at her candor. Apparently, Lucy didn't sugarcoat things. But neither did her brother.

"I don't plan on taking him. I plan on honoring Sammy's wishes. She wanted him to know his father. She just never got around to..."

Loss hit her again, the way it often did.

Lucy briefly touched her shoulder. The gesture was sweet, but Lissa knew that the other woman wouldn't switch loyalties. And neither could Lissa. She'd made a promise, to do what was best for Oliver. Somehow she'd thought it would be easier. She thought she'd show up and find a man unfit to parent. What she'd found was a man who hadn't planned to parent, but a man who was loyal and caring. It made the whole process so much harder than she'd expected.

"Marcus is a good man," Lucy defended. "None of us are without baggage, without a past. But few men will defend or care for their loved ones the way my brother does."

"I understand you feel strongly about your brother. But Oliver..." She nearly choked on the emotion that welled up from her heart.

Lucy's expression softened with understanding. "What was Sammy like?"

"Not perfect. She had her baggage and her past."

"What was she like as a mother?"

"She struggled." Lissa looked down at the tile floor. "But she loved her little boy."

"I'm sure she did. But I'm also sure that you love him, too."

"I do." She swiped at her eyes and gave herself a minute to get her emotions under control. "I don't want to hurt Marcus. But I also don't want Oliver to be hurt."

"Then I guess we both want the same thing. I just hope that you'll give Marcus a chance."

Give Marcus a chance. Lissa wished it didn't sound as if Lucy was connecting her to Oliver's father. It wasn't about her feelings for him. Because she didn't have feelings for him. She was there to introduce Oliver to his father. A man she would probably see from time to time, but they wouldn't be connected in any way.

Period.

A few minutes later she had to remind herself of that belief. Marcus had arrived and he'd taken a seat with Oliver and an older gentleman Lissa didn't know. He buttered a biscuit for his son and must have known she was watching. With a smile he made eye contact with her.

She told herself again, no connection. Nothing happened when he smiled and winked like that. She didn't feel a thing. Because she wouldn't feel anything. Jane had told her to wait because someday the right man would convince her that he was worth her time. The right man would be a partner. He wouldn't control. He wouldn't take over. He wouldn't hurt her with his hands or his words.

The right man would make her feel as if the future with him at her side mattered, that it made sense.

She could trust herself because she would know that man when he stepped into her life.

It would be the right time, the right man, the right place. Not this man, this place or this time. Even if there was something about Marcus Palermo, the way he helped his son at the buffet line, the way he stopped to talk to the older people, taking time, truly listening. He didn't believe himself to be good enough to be a little boy's father. If she was going to lose

Oliver to him, she knew she would have to help him to realize he could be the person his son needed.

They were not a team, but they were two people who cared about a young boy. It mattered that they could get along.

She could see good in him. She wasn't so naive that she couldn't also see that he was charming, and her ability to resist him seemed limited.

A man who was kind to his son, to the elderly and to animals. It was a lethal combination.

Chapter Seven

Water rolled over the top of the bridge Marcus had crossed more times than he could count. He hit the brakes and stopped his truck. Next to him, Lissa looked a little bit nervous. He glanced in the back seat of his truck and smiled at Oliver. The boy didn't have a clue. In five-year-old fashion he was talking to a toy he'd brought along for the ride to church.

"I guess we won't be going this way." He stated the obvious.

He guessed Essie, who had left earlier for Sunday services, must have taken the back route to town. He dialed her number as he backed away from the bridge. When she answered, he felt a serious sense of relief.

"Making sure you're okay."

His aunt sighed. "Well, I guess I have enough sense not to cross a low-water bridge.

And I already told first responders. They are on their way out with barricades. I took the county line road to get to town. It's about the only way."

"We'll be late for church," he told her and Lissa at the same time.

A few minutes later they were on the best route to town. It would take an extra ten minutes, but at least they'd get there safely. When they finally pulled into the church parking lot, it was packed. Definitely more than the usual Sunday crowd. Probably several people staying in the shelter the church had set up. Others were there to pray that the rain would stop.

Lissa's phone dinged. A text this time and not a call. He watched as she peeked at the phone and slipped it back in her purse. She'd done that several times. He didn't like games. Even if it didn't concern him, he wanted to know the truth. He wanted, for her sake and Oliver's, to know that she was safe.

"Going to ignore it again?" he asked, realizing that might have sounded a tinge jealous. He hadn't planned on jealousy, but for some reason he seemed to feel responsible for the woman who had been taking care of his son.

Responsible. Yes, much easier than thinking of himself as jealous.

"I'm not ignoring anything," she answered. "And it isn't any of your business."

Lissa tossed her head toward the back seat, as if warning him the conversation was off-limits with the child in the truck. He was starting to think that was her way of avoiding any conversation she didn't feel comfortable with.

He wanted to talk about those phone calls because she had to have a reason for ignoring them. Either she didn't want him to hear her talk to her boyfriend or she was hiding something else. He might be late to fatherhood, but it mattered that his son and the woman caring for him were both safe.

"We're going to discuss this," he said as he pulled his keys from the ignition.

"Nope." She got out of the truck and opened the back door for Oliver. The boy hadn't said much since they'd left Essie's. As a matter of fact, he hadn't said too much since yesterday. Mostly he gave them both some serious questioning looks, and he seemed a little bit upset.

Marcus got the feeling they needed to talk to Oliver, tell him what the situation was and let him adjust. No more of this taking time, letting him get settled.

As they headed up the sidewalk, Oliver hurried ahead of them, still clutching the toy he'd had in the truck.

"We have to tell him."

Lissa faltered at his words and he reached for her arm, steadying her. "Right. I know we do. I just wanted to give it time."

"I think we don't have a lot of time. I know you want to take him back to San Antonio with you. And I know full well that with Sammy's letter and her will, you feel as if you have that right. But he's my son. I'm going to make some decisions that you might not like. The first one is that we need to tell him. Soon. And you have to understand that I won't let you walk away with him, not without a fight."

So much for the cowboy who wasn't sure if he was ready to be a dad. He hadn't been sure. He still wasn't all the way in, but he also wasn't going to let his son down. Walking away from Oliver would definitely be letting him down.

Her careful gaze shifted to his face, to the scar on his cheek. "I guess we know where we both stand."

"I guess we do."

He started toward the church, knowing she had a hurt expression on her face and tears swimming in her blue eyes. He'd spent a lifetime being cold, shutting out his feelings, pretending he didn't care. He tried to call on all of the tactics he'd learned over a lifetime of finding it easier to not feel. It might have worked if their fingers hadn't brushed as they walked. The cold and standoffish routine was difficult to achieve when you noticed a woman's tears and you were tempted to reach for her hand.

"Stop looking at me like that," she warned as they climbed the steps. "You don't have to worry. I'm not going to fall apart."

He blinked back his surprise. He didn't go around with his heart on his sleeve or emotion in his eyes. He was the ice man, that was what they had called him when he rode bulls. Nothing scared him. He had faced the meanest bulls in the world and he'd conquered them. But this woman could take him to his knees, she made him want to protect her.

"If you keep looking at me like that, people will get the wrong idea." She poked at his arm.

He rubbed the spot and grimaced. "Sorry. I really don't want to hurt you, Lissa. Would it be better if I said something about how good you smell?"

Reaching for the handrail, he headed up the steps, taking them slower than he would have liked. He looked back and she was standing at the bottom of the steps, hand over her heart.

"Was that a compliment?"

He shook his head. "Nope."

"You're just trying to make me smile. Right?"

He glanced inside the sanctuary and raised a finger to his lips. "They're praying."

He eased into a pew and scooted to make room for Lissa. Oliver had found a seat a few pews in front, with Lucy, her husband, Dane Scott, and their daughter Issy.

Next to him, Lissa's hand stole to his and her fingers, soft and feminine, curled around his roughly calloused ones. She gave a light squeeze and bowed her head, her lips moving softly as she prayed.

Thread by complicated thread she was undoing his resolve, his plans and his composure. She made it difficult to sit through that sermon and keep his mind focused. Somehow, though, he managed to pray for guidance, because he knew the coming weeks wouldn't be easy. They could all be hurt in the process of figuring out what would be best for Oliver.

After church they stood and made their way forward, to Oliver and to the rest of his family.

"You must have slipped in after we started." Lucy smiled from him to Lissa. "Lissa, I think Doc is looking for you. Something about setting up a clinic here at the church and he might need your help. I think he has a little bit of a crush on you."

Marcus ignored that comment. But then he couldn't ignore his little sister Maria. She came barreling up the aisle, nineteen and still the most exuberant member of the family. She wrapped her arms around him and hugged tight.

"Hug me back, Marc." She gave him another squeeze.

He did his best not to stiffen in her embrace. She was a hugger and nothing he said could ever stop her.

"Don't call me Marc," he grumbled at her. "Welcome home, squirt."

"You even sound like you mean it."

He did mean it, but he decided not to encourage her. "When did you get home?"

"Early this morning. It took me forever to get here, avoiding flooded roads and bridges."

"She brought a friend with her," Lucy interjected. "His name is Jake."

Maria gave her a look and kept talking.

"I met Oliver." Maria gave him what passed as her serious look. "He's a cutie. Chip off the old block, but a lot more charming."

"Quiet," he ordered.

"Chip off the old block," Lissa repeated. "That's another one we could use."

"Stop." He couldn't help but give in to the smile that tugged at his lips.

"Was that a smile?" Maria stepped closer

and peered at him. "I think it might have been. Have I been gone that long?"

"You've been gone long enough that you brought a friend home to meet the family," Lucy interjected, with a look at Marcus that meant she was sparing him their little sister's questions by distracting her.

"So where is this friend?" Marcus surveyed the room and didn't see anyone unfamiliar.

"Helping stack sandbags in front of Essie's." Maria slipped her arm through his. Concern darkened her eyes. "How are you doing?"

"I'm fine." He didn't pull away, but he was aware that his younger sister always knew him a little better than anyone.

"They're serving lunch in the fellowship hall. I have to find my crew." Lucy shot him a look, as if to make sure he followed her meaning. "You should find Oliver. I think he went with Dane to get Jewel from the nursery."

He hadn't thought about Oliver. Another point against him. A dad should think about his child, know where he was, consider his well-being. Things like food were important.

"Come with me." Lissa took him by the arm. "I'm here for two more weeks, Marcus. I'm not going to leave you to sink or swim."

He was obviously drowning, but he wasn't about to tell that to the woman at his side. Not when the drowning had as much to do with her as it did trying to figure out how to be a father. Both had him in over his head, out of his depth and a few other sayings he could think of. Sink or swim, she'd said. She had no idea how fitting that was for his current state of mind.

Lissa clasped her hands behind her back as they walked down the hallway in the direction of the nursery. The church, once the church where Jesse Palermo had pastored, was now a shelter for abused women as well as a community church. Several of the classrooms had been turned into dorms for those seeking a way to build a new life. With the threat of flooding, single women from the community were being offered cots in the living areas.

It was symbolic in so many ways. The church Marcus's dad pastored had left broken lives behind, and this church was rebuilding lives and the community. Lissa admired Marcus—it had to take a lot of strength to put that behind him and to be there helping. She'd learned that he gave to the mission of the church and also helped with construction projects.

People had been forthcoming with more information about Marcus and the Palermos than she really needed. She realized that some were trying to give her advice and others thought there might be something between her and the remaining single Palermo twin.

Some less helpful folks had told her about Marcus's years of alcoholism and how he used to turn to the bottle when life got tense. She thought they were more interested in stirring up trouble than in truly helping.

But she hadn't ignored their carefully veiled warnings. A man who had once stayed drunk more than he stayed sober. Could he take care of Oliver? What if he turned back to his old ways?

Several feet from the door, Marcus stopped, his expression unreadable, his eyes cool and detached. Or that was what a person might think if they didn't look too closely. In the past week she'd learned a little about how to read him. She saw that he was never really without emotion. He might not smile and laugh, but the feelings were there, beneath the surface. And what she saw right now was a man afraid of how his life had changed.

"What in the world am I doing?" he asked, his raspy voice gruff.

"Becoming a dad," she challenged.

His gaze darted to the door at the end of the hall. The nursery. She could see that he was torn.

"This is crazy." He yanked off his cowboy hat and brushed a hand through his hair.

"It isn't," she encouraged. That hadn't been the role she'd expected to take in this situation, that of encourager. She hadn't wanted to trust this man or cheer him on.

Especially when he'd made it clear he would fight for his son. She knew if it came to it he would take her to court. And he would win.

"You came here hoping to find me unable to care for my son. You were probably right in believing that, so don't start acting supportive now."

"We should get Oliver. They're serving lunch."

They entered the nursery and she watched with a pang of envy as Marcus lowered himself to the floor to sit with his son. They talked about the toys, about Lucy's little girls, Jewel and Issy, whose father had already taken them to the fellowship hall. And then Oliver mentioned a pig that sometimes ran through town and he wondered if he would ever see that pig.

Marcus guaranteed him he would. Lissa wanted to tell him that adults didn't make promises they weren't sure they would be able to keep.

But she didn't have a chance. Marcus swooped his son up into his arms and told him it was time for lunch. Before she could object, he had the little boy on his shoulders. Oliver pulled the hat off Marcus's head and placed it on his own. "Can I stay up here?"

Lissa started to protest, but it came out as a squeak. Marcus glanced at her, amusement dancing in his dark eyes for a brief few seconds.

She shrugged, because she wasn't going to be the naysayer. Marcus turned his head a bit to look at his son.

"You'll have to duck or you'll hit your head as we go out the door."

"I can do that," Oliver assured them.

They entered the fellowship hall, Oliver laughing as Marcus told him about a summer picnic at the church complete with bounce houses.

"We don't have to go home yet, do we?" the boy asked as Marcus lifted him from his shoulders and placed him back on the floor. The white cowboy hat covered his eyes and he pushed it back to look up at them.

"No, not yet," Lissa assured him.

People were going through a line, filling plates with food. Oliver didn't hesitate. He left them and headed for the food line.

"This is why we need to tell him."

She sighed. He was right…she needed to tell him. It just hadn't been her plan to get stuck here. She hadn't planned to witness the child she'd been raising become attached to the man who was his father. She didn't know what she'd expected. She'd loaded Oliver up and told him she had someone she wanted him to meet.

"This can't continue," he whispered close to her ear.

"I know, Marcus. I do know." Lissa was aware now that Oliver was talking to Pastor Matthews. She smiled at what she saw. "Look at him."

"What?" Marcus asked.

"The way he's standing. He's so much like you. Even down to the way he stands and the way he talks."

Marcus glanced from her to his son and a corner of his mouth quirked up. "Yeah, chip off the old block. Pretty cute kid."

The tension of moments ago evaporated.

"If you do say so yourself," she teased.

At that, a full grin spread across his face, revealing dimples she'd never noticed before. And that grin slayed her. She hadn't expected the power behind his smile, the way it changed him. She cleared her throat, uncomfortable with the thought, the way that smile tugged at something deep inside her.

One minute he had her convinced he couldn't possibly be responsible enough to be a father, and the next moment she wanted to help him achieve that goal.

"Are you okay?"

"Of course I am," she assured him. "You should help him with his plate."

He gave her a knowing look.

"I get that he's everything to you." He placed a hand on her shoulder. "This is a mess, you know. We can't undo the past, but it shouldn't have been like this. I didn't want to be my father. I should have been there five years ago. I should have been there last year. You could have called me."

When Sammy died. Lissa closed her eyes briefly, feeling guilty because she should have called him. She should have allowed him to be there for Sammy, for Oliver. Instead, she'd listened to her sister, granted her the last wish and promised to see this plan through to the end. Lissa should have known it would cause them all more pain in the end.

"I am sorry," she told him. "I should have called you when she had the accident."

"But you didn't," he said, and then seemed to become aware of their surroundings. The hurt, the anger, all of the emotions that had flitted across his face suddenly disappeared. From a distance, anyone would think he didn't care, that he wasn't affected.

However, she knew the truth. It was in the dark depths of his eyes. The pain of the past, the anger, the confusion.

"I'll get him a plate. And you. Go sit down and I'll bring you one, too." He gave her a brief quirk of the lips, his version of a smile. "Step one in becoming a father. Kids have to eat."

"No peas. Oliver doesn't like peas."

"Neither do I."

Unwittingly, she had given them a connection. Of course, half the little boys, and maybe grown men, across the country would say the same about peas. She could have added that she didn't like them, either.

But she didn't.

Maria, the youngest of the Palermo siblings, waved at her from a table in the corner. She was seated with Lucy's stepdaughter, Issy, and with the little girl Lucy and her husband, Dane, had adopted, Jewel. The child, eighteen months old, was Maria's biological child whom she'd asked her older sister to raise. The Palermo kids had been through a lot, but what Lissa saw was a family that had begun the healing process and they had a lot of love for one another.

Her foster parents had given Lissa and Sammy that family bond. They were the grandparents of Oliver. They were the home they went to for holidays. They were the people Lissa counted on, even now.

She sat down at the table with Maria, who was busy cutting meat and helping Issy, blind since birth, with her food.

"Can I help?" Lissa offered.

Maria flashed her an amused look. "That's very brave of you. But of course you can help. With these two, we always accept help. If you can make sure Jewel keeps her food on the tray of that high chair and not the floor, that would be great. Is Marcus bringing you a plate?"

"He is." She looked away, uncomfortable with the questions she saw forming in Maria's eyes. Questions about Marcus. About her relationship to him.

She was here because Sammy wasn't. Sammy, who had gone to the store to pick up a few things while Lissa watched Oliver and had died in a car accident. She'd lived long enough to tell Lissa to give Marcus a chance to be a dad.

If Sammy had lived, would the two of them, Marcus and Sammy, have found each other again? Would they have been a family?

"That's about the sweetest picture ever," Maria spoke, catching her attention and thankfully distracting her.

She followed the younger woman's gaze and

had to agree. Marcus had a tray and was heading their way. Next to him, still wearing Marcus's hat, Oliver carried his own tray. They were talking, with Marcus leaning down to catch what his son had to say.

"Yes, the sweetest." Lissa could admit the cowboy made it easy to drop her guard. She had to keep things in check and remember that this man had a history of leaving broken hearts in his wake.

She hoped and prayed that Marcus Palermo could be the father Oliver deserved. And she also prayed that her heart wouldn't be shattered beyond repair in the process.

Chapter Eight

One thing Marcus really disliked was being the center of attention. With Oliver tagging along next to him as they made their way to the table, they were getting plenty of attention. An arm bumped his and he sidestepped before realizing it was Lucy.

"Calm down, it's just me. And get that cornered look off your face." Trust his older sister to see right through him and not give him space.

"I don't like crowds." There, that ought to keep her out of his business.

Instead, she gave him a curious look that bordered on maternal. Oliver had left them. He was pulling out a chair and setting his tray on the table. Lissa leaned to listen to something he said.

Lucy cleared her throat to get his attention.

"Marcus, if you need anything…if you need to talk, I'm here." Lucy, now the family therapist, stood on tiptoe and kissed his cheek. He'd been right about that maternal look softening her expression.

"Who are you?" he mumbled, and she didn't seem at all troubled by the question. Instead, she gave him a parting grin and headed for the table.

Of course, he wouldn't escape her. Her daughters were at the table with Maria and Lissa.

He ought to ask if there was going to be another little one at the family table next spring. That would get her off his back. And then he realized he liked the idea of another baby at their holiday table.

He'd learned something about himself in the past six months or so. He did like babies. He liked kids. And with that thought, his gaze shifted to Oliver. His son. It got him in the solar plexus, whatever that was. It felt safer than saying it affected his heart.

"I got you a plate." He set it down in front of Lissa, ignoring Lucy. "Oliver assured me you like lasagna. He also told me to get you a double helping of peas. I didn't."

She tickled Oliver and then kissed his cheek.

"He would do that to me. Thank you for not listening to him."

Across the table from them, Lucy made a choking sound. Marcus glanced at her, but she pretended to be helping Issy with her food. It was new, this teasing version of his sister.

Lucy had found some happiness. And peace. It was written all over her face, shone from her eyes.

He guessed that was what all the Palermo siblings wanted, for the others to be happy. And Lucy was happy. He searched the room for Alex, because Marcus's twin had found the same for himself. Who could have known that picking up a bride on the side of the road would work out so well for a man?

"Can I have my chocolate cake now?" Oliver asked as he pushed green beans around his plate.

Marcus glanced at Lissa to see what she would say, but she arched a brow, returning the question to him. He looked at his son's plate, still filled with chicken, vegetables and mashed potatoes.

"I think you have to eat at least part of the good food before you get dessert," Marcus answered. "Now, I'm just guessing at that, but I know that I always eat my dinner before I tackle dessert. You won't get strong eating cake."

"If I eat ten bites of each thing?" Oliver looked pretty hopeful, and ten bites of each thing would pretty much clean his plate.

"I think that's a deal." Marcus poured ketchup on his own mashed potatoes and ignored the look Lissa gave him, a pretty disgusted look if he was to guess.

He wasn't going to explain to her about a real dislike for mashed potatoes. When he was a kid, they were required to eat everything on their plate. Ketchup, he'd discovered, made some foods go down a little easier.

He was finishing up when the outside door flew open and a first responder rushed in carrying a child. Throughout the fellowship hall, people froze, their gazes glued to the scene, the man in his yellow vest, the child, pale and unmoving. Next to Marcus, Lissa moved quickly to her feet and hurried toward the scene that everyone else suddenly seemed to understand. People rose. Many murmured. Marcus hoped they were praying, because the child, a little girl, didn't look good.

"Watch Oliver," he said to Maria as he pushed back from the table. She nodded, her eyes large as she watched Lissa hurrying through the room with the first responder.

Marcus followed them down the hall to Doc's makeshift clinic. He stopped at the door and watched as Lissa leaned over the child, who appeared to be a year or two older than Oliver. It got him in the gut, watching that little girl and thinking about his own son.

Lissa had a stethoscope and she helped the child to sit as she listened to her heart, her breaths. Tears were streaming down the child's face.

"My mommy?" She leaned into Lissa's shoulder.

Marcus made eye contact with the first responder, who shook his head only slightly before answering. "We're looking for her."

No promise that she would be okay or that they would find her. Marcus knew what had happened. The wet clothes of the child, the search. The mom must have driven through water and she hadn't gauged the depth or the power behind the swiftly moving force. He wanted to go help search. He should be helping.

"Marcus, could you find Doc? And if the two of you will leave, Pearl and I will find her some dry clothes to change into. We'll need blankets, too. And a heating pad if you can find one. Her temp is low."

"The water was cold." Pearl shuddered as she spoke and then her teeth started to chatter.

Marcus grabbed a pile of blankets and

handed them over to Lissa. "I'll see what I can find."

"I want my mommy." The little girl was full-on crying now. And Marcus wasn't good with tears. It brought back too many memories.

"I'll be back."

The first responder followed him from the room. "Doc is at the search site. In case they do find the mom."

Marcus wanted to spew just about every curse word he'd ever been paddled for saying. And then some. Instead, he stopped and said a quick prayer that they'd find Pearl's mommy.

"How'd they get the little girl out?"

"Her mom got her out the window. She told us she grabbed a branch, but the car went under. I don't think we'll find her mom alive."

"Family?"

"Not from around here. They were on their way to Oklahoma, where the mom has family."

Marcus went from wanting to say some strong words to wanting to hit something. "Okay, let's see if we can find out the name of those relatives and give them a call."

The dining room had cleared out except for the Palermo family and a few others. Pastor Matthews stood in the little group and he clearly didn't have good news. His face paled and he shook his head.

"Did they find her?" the first responder asked.

"They're still looking, Joe," Pastor Matthews assured him. "They found the car and she wasn't inside. So that gives us hope that she got out."

"I pray she did. That little girl is about the age of my Sara." Joe brushed at his eyes. "Okay, I have to get back to work."

"Let's pray before you go," Pastor Matthews offered. Joe took off his hat and Marcus joined the two men. As the pastor prayed, a few others joined their circle.

After praying, Marcus searched for Oliver, who was a short distance away, tears swimming in his dark eyes.

"What's up, buddy?" Marcus squatted to put himself at eye level with his son.

"That girl's mom died?" Oliver was sobbing now, tears streaming down his cheeks. And Lissa wasn't there. Lissa the comforter. It wasn't what Marcus did. He was an action man. He wanted to solve the problem, not look it face on.

"No, kiddo, they're still looking for her and we just prayed that they would find her." Because he couldn't lie to his son. "And the little girl is okay. Her mom saved her."

"But her mom might not come back."

"I think she will," Marcus told his son. Then

it hit him that Oliver was thinking about his own lost mommy.

He stood, and as he did, he picked Oliver up and held him close. Little arms wrapped around his neck.

"I'm sorry, Oliver." Sorry he hadn't been there for his son. Sorry that Sammy was gone. And sorry that he was a rotten excuse for a human being.

As much as Marcus didn't believe he was fit to be anyone's father, he realized he needed to be the man his son could count on.

"I miss her." Oliver didn't cry anymore; he just held on tight and let Marcus carry him from the room. His family didn't stop them and didn't ask questions.

Marcus didn't know what else to do. He wanted to comfort his son. He wanted to make things right for him and for the little girl down the hall. Life wasn't fair. Sometimes it took some real skill to get over the past, the hurts, the failures.

"I want Lissa," Oliver said softly, his cheek against Marcus's shoulder. Marcus had been thinking almost the same thing. Lissa had become his anchor, too.

He didn't want to add her to the list of people he had failed.

"We'll give her a few minutes and then we'll

see her." He started to put Oliver down, but the boy held on tight to his neck.

"No."

"Okay, little man, I'll carry you."

They stopped at the door to the clinic. He could hear Lissa's soft voice. He heard a child sobbing and Pastor Matthews saying something gentle and comforting. He continued to hold Oliver as they stood outside the door.

The door opened and Lissa stepped out. She swiped at her eyes and then somehow managed a smile. "Hey, you two."

"Did they find her mommy?" Oliver asked. "If she's sad, I could let her play with my toy truck."

Lissa leaned in to kiss Oliver. "That's very sweet of you. We found her a teddy bear and she's resting now. They're still looking for her mom."

"We prayed they would find her." Oliver reached for Lissa. She took him, holding him tight.

Marcus knew that expression. She needed the hug as much as the little boy needed it. Sighing at the realization, he stepped close and wrapped them both in his arms. Surprisingly, it wasn't bad. Especially when Lissa relaxed in his embrace, snuggling close.

He'd spent a lot of time chasing after fame

on the bull-riding circuit, chasing wealth and even chasing women. However, he'd never experienced what that moment brought to him. Right here, right now, he felt like the person they needed.

"Thank you." She stood on tiptoe and kissed his cheek.

Just like that, she undid his calm. She rocked his world a little. It was the simplest thing on the planet, a kiss on the cheek. But it wasn't simple. Coffee was simple. A sunrise fell into that category. Maybe even a quiet evening on the porch. But a kiss from Lissa—that complicated things.

Lissa had needed his presence and the hug he had offered. His embrace had seemed something of a sacrifice. It wasn't like him to give of himself that way. That made it all the more special.

"You all should go. It will be getting late. Oliver needs a bath and clean clothes. He'll need dinner and a bedtime story."

The demands put them back on firm footing. She could see it in Marcus's eyes.

"I think those are things you should do."

She laughed a little. "You can manage. You run the water. Make sure it isn't too hot or too cold. He can handle the washing and dressing parts. But then it's story time. This is why I'm here…"

She didn't finish because Oliver eyed her curiously. He didn't know what to think of her turning his care over to someone who had been a stranger just a few days ago.

"Right. Okay, we can do this." Marcus gave her a long look. "You'll call if you hear something?"

"I'll call." If she heard something about Pearl's mother. That was what he meant.

They left and it wasn't easy, watching them walk away together. They were bonding. She told herself that was the way it should be. But her other self argued with that because she didn't want to lose Oliver. She didn't want to honor the letter Sammy had left.

It just wasn't fair. Her foster sister had given birth to Oliver, but she had neglected him and left his care to Lissa. She should have a say in who would raise him. She leaned against the wall and took deep breaths to get past the anger and the hurt.

Several hours after Pearl had been brought to the clinic, Doc Parker returned.

"Lissa, I'm glad as anything to see you here. And how is our little patient?"

Pearl had fallen asleep. Her tearstained cheeks were pale, and she sometimes cried a little as if she dreamed of the accident that had pulled their car into the water. But she was otherwise unharmed. Lissa put a finger to her mouth and pointed to the child.

"Sleeping. They're trying to get a state caseworker here, but with the roads…"

"Ah," Doc whispered. "She's a cute little thing. No idea where she is from or where they were heading?"

"None."

He shook his head and eased closer to the bed to study the child. "We'll keep praying."

"Of course we will," Lissa responded.

Doc eyed Lissa over the top of his wire-framed glasses. "So, do you plan on letting Marcus be a part of the boy's life?"

Of course everyone had guessed. It wasn't a stretch. When a person saw Oliver and Marcus together, it was obvious they were father and son.

"Yes, he'll be a part of Oliver's life. As much as he wants to be a part of his life."

Doc raised his glasses to the top of his head and gave her a look that could only be disappointment. "Don't let his gruff demeanor fool you. Marcus Palermo cares. Deeply. He's loyal to a fault. And he isn't going to just let you walk away with his son."

She knew that. A month ago she had convinced herself that the cowboy Sammy had described was the type of man who wouldn't want to deal with a child. She'd convinced herself he would just sign over custody. It had been easy to believe. Until she met him. Now, although she wasn't sure of his parenting ability, she was positive he would fight for his son.

"His voice?" she asked. She needed to change the subject, and she did wonder about Marcus and what had happened to him during his childhood.

"That's his story to tell."

"Because Marcus loves to talk about himself," she said.

At that, Doc laughed. "Yes, he's a talker."

They both knew that he wasn't.

Doc got up to pour himself a cup of coffee. "Oliver's mom died in a car accident?"

"Yes, she did."

"That's a tough one. And you're a good woman for being there for him. I guess you could always stay in Bluebonnet. Maybe the two of you could work out a custody agreement."

"I have a job in San Antonio."

"Of course you do. But change isn't always bad. And if it's a job you're worried about, I could use a good nurse."

Stay in Bluebonnet? No, she couldn't imagine herself living in a small town. She had never considered leaving San Antonio. She loved her job. Her foster parents and friends were in San Antonio.

But if Marcus took custody of Oliver, her heart would be here. In Bluebonnet Springs.

"I don't think so, Doc. I'm just here for two more weeks."

He let out a sigh. "I'm sorry to hear that. How is it you're related to Oliver?"

"His mother and I were foster children in the same home."

"That's a tough situation." He sat on a rolling stool and faced her. "I'm sure this won't be easy for any of you."

"No, it won't be."

"Well, I know you probably have a lot of opportunities in the city, but I'm going to leave the offer on the table and hope you'll reconsider. I could use a good nurse practitioner to run the clinic when I retire."

"I appreciate that offer. And I'm not qualified as a nurse practitioner."

"It's something to work toward."

It was an offer she never would have expected. It was an open door if she needed one. She could stay in Oliver's life. She would also be stuck in Marcus's life. And Oliver's daddy was becoming problematic for more reasons than the one she had anticipated.

He was not the person Sammy had described. He controlled his temper, spoke gently to his son, and he cared deeply about the people in his life.

For the past few days he had made her feel like one of those people.

Chapter Nine

At nine o'clock, Marcus handed Oliver his toothbrush and his bear pajamas. He had to admit, he was proud of himself. He'd kept his son safe for an entire day, fed him, spent time with him, and now he was rocking the bedtime routine.

"Do you have a step stool?" Oliver stood at the bathroom sink, eyeing it with a look that said he didn't see this happening.

"Let me ask Essie," Marcus offered. He looked from the sink to the boy. "Or I can pick you up and set you on the counter."

Oliver looked at the granite top and nodded. "Okay, lift me up."

Marcus lifted Oliver, who then sat crossed-legged on the granite vanity top to brush his teeth. When he finished, he jumped back down and reached for a washcloth to wipe his face. Marcus watched, amused at the bed-time routine.

"Will you read me a story?" Oliver asked as he put the brush back in the drawer. "Lissa always reads to me."

"What does she read?" he asked, watching as Oliver brushed his hair, almost as if he meant to go out and not to bed. When he finished, he handed the brush to Marcus.

"She reads the bible storybook to me. And *The Three Little Pigs*. Do you like *The Three Little Pigs*?" Oliver reached for his hand.

Marcus took that small hand in his. Did Oliver miss Sammy? That was a stupid question. Of course he missed his mom. Marcus's own mother had skated out on her family. Even though Marcus had been a teen and he'd understood why she left, he'd missed her.

And resented her. But she'd never read to him.

"So? Will you read me a story?" Oliver asked as he led Marcus to his bedroom.

A room the little boy obviously shared with Lissa. There were twin beds covered with handmade quilts. A rocking chair held folded clothes. And the room smelled of citrus and wildflowers. Lissa's perfume, if he was to guess.

"I'll tell you a story," Marcus offered.

He pulled back the blankets on one of the beds, the one with a stuffed teddy bear and a dinosaur robot that didn't look too cuddly. He moved the dinosaur to the dresser and sat down on the edge of the bed as Oliver slid under the quilt. The little boy, eyes sleepy and big, reached for the teddy bear.

"What story will you tell me?" Oliver asked on a yawn.

"I like the story of God's people praising Him as they went against the enemy. There weren't very many of them, but God promised them the victory if the priests went before them singing praises."

"Did they win?" Oliver asked, his eyes getting heavy.

"They did win."

"Will you pray?" Oliver opened one eye. "I'm kind of sleepy. Pray they find that lady. And will you tell God to tell my mom that I'm okay."

"I will."

Marcus was glad Oliver's eyes were closed, because those prayer requests hit him hard. He brushed away the tear that trickled down his son's cheek and felt one slip free from his own eye. He might not be much of a dad, but it hadn't taken him long to realize he loved his son. If it took a fight, he would have Oliver in his life.

He prayed a silent prayer for all of them, and then he prayed for Oliver and for Lissa and the town. He tagged on the special request that God pass on a message to Sammy. Oliver was okay. He was better than okay. He had people who loved him and they were looking out for him.

There was no echoing amen at the end of the prayer. Oliver had rolled over onto his side, the bear tucked close to his chin, his thumb in his mouth.

"Good night, son." He tucked the comforter around Oliver, then left the room, flipping off the light as he went.

Essie was sitting in the living room working on a quilt. She glanced up as he walked in, and then she removed the glasses she wore for close-up work and reading.

"What are you going to do?" she asked.

"I'm not sure. I mean, I know I'm going to be his dad. I'm not sure how to take him from Lissa. She's been his mother for the past year, but she's also been in his life since the day he was born."

"I think you'll figure it out. You're already figuring it out."

"I'm glad you think that, but this was just

one night. We're talking a lifetime of nights."
A lifetime of opportunities to let his son down.
He checked his watch. "I should go get Lissa."

"You be careful on those roads, Marcus. I've
been listening to the scanner and it's treacher-
ous. Accident after accident tonight. And the
water is coming up fast."

"I'll be careful. Anything you need from
town?"

She shook her head. "Not that I can think
of. Let me know when you get home. Even if
I'm sleeping, wake me up."

"I'll wake you up when I bring Lissa, but
then I'm going on back to my place."

She had her glasses back on, but she raised
them a fraction to give him a forbidding look.
"You can't sleep there tonight. If the water
comes up, I'm sorry, but it might take out that
old farmhouse."

"It's been standing a long time, Essie." He
couldn't imagine the farmhouse being gone.
Most of his good memories were built around
that house and the Browns.

She continued to give him a look.

He bent to kiss the top of her head. "I'll stay
at Alex's."

"Good."

She went back to quilting and he headed out
the back door to his truck.

The rain appeared to be coming down even harder, if that was possible. It took him twenty minutes to make the ten-minute drive to town. When he pulled into the church lot, a patrol car was leaving. He parked and jumped out of his truck, running for the nearest door of the church and avoiding puddles along the way. Pastor Matthews must have seen him coming, because he had the door open as Marcus rushed up the steps.

"Come into the ark," the pastor said as Marcus entered the building, swiping a hand over his face to wipe away the rain.

"Why's the county cop here?" Marcus asked as he shrugged out of his rain-soaked jacket.

"We had a little incident with a spouse. Your friend is a black belt. Did you know that?"

"My friend?"

Duncan Matthews grinned. Marcus liked the pastor. He considered him a friend. One of his few. But the look on his face might move him from the friend category.

"Oh, come on, Marcus, have a sense of humor."

"I have a sense of humor," he grumbled. "Is she okay?"

"You mean Lissa? The woman who isn't your friend?" Pastor Matthews nodded and they started down the hall together. "She's fine. Slow down and try not to charge back there like you think the building is on fire. She did take a blow to the jaw, but she says it isn't broken, just bruised. Doc says she's done for the night and needs to go home and get some rest."

"That's why I'm here, to take her home." He stumbled over that last word and heat crawled into his cheeks. "To take her to Essie's."

They entered the clinic and he spotted her sitting in a rocking chair, legs drawn up, an ice pack on her cheek. She sighed when she saw him, as if she knew him well enough to know what he might be thinking or what he might say.

The last thing he planned to do was say what he was thinking. He thought she looked small, sitting in the chair curled up like that. He thought she looked like a woman who needed a hug. And he wasn't a hugger. Maybe Essie could give her a hug. Or Oliver.

Not him.

Hugging her was the last thing he wanted to do.

"You heard?" she asked when he pulled up a stool and sat next to her.

"Yeah, I heard. You're okay?"

"Yeah, I'm okay. I should have been more observant. If I'd been on my guard, I would have noticed, but I thought I could defuse the situation with words. I prefer words."

"Black belt?"

Blue eyes twinkled at him. "Yeah. Surprise. My foster mom wanted me to feel empowered."

He understood that. What he didn't understand was why he reached to move the ice pack. He didn't get why he needed to see where she'd been struck. He definitely didn't understand why he touched the bruised flesh and felt the pain deep, as if it were his own.

He closed his eyes against memories that called to mind why he cared. He knew why it mattered. He knew why it bothered him to see her flesh marred, to see the flash of pain in her eyes. He and his siblings had all suffered at the hands of their father.

"Stop. You didn't do this."

How had she known his thoughts? Did she guess that he always feared the monster deep within? What if it was sleeping, waiting to someday rear its ugly head and lash out at someone he cared about? He'd lost his temper once with Sammy. He'd called the next day and told her they were done. Not because of her, but because of him. He wouldn't allow himself to get close if it meant he might hurt someone he cared about.

"No, I didn't do this," he answered gruffly. "Let's get you back to Essie's so you can sleep. Doc, I'm taking your patient home. Need anything before we go?"

Doc looked up from the desk he'd commandeered. He glanced from Lissa to Marcus. "No, I don't need anything. I am sorry that you're taking my assistant. I guess you won't be able to talk her into staying and working with me on a permanent basis."

Lissa stay permanently in Bluebonnet? She had stepped away from him and was studying the little girl, who still slept on the bed. Her lips moved in a silent prayer. A woman of faith. Something else to like about her.

No, he didn't think he could talk her into staying. And he wasn't sure he wanted to. "Sorry, Doc, you're on your own."

He glanced at the woman standing next to him. She looked about done in and she was cradling her arm, probably to give her shoulder some relief. When her time was up in a couple of weeks, she'd probably be glad to see the last of Bluebonnet.

Until then, he guessed it was up to him to take care of her. He would put her in the category of family. That would make it easier to deal with whatever it was he felt.

* * *

They were walking down the hall when Marcus stopped abruptly. Lissa glanced up at him, wondering what was going on. He was always the strong, silent type, but since he'd arrived at the church to take her home, he'd gone beyond silent.

Brooding might be a better word.

"What?" she asked as he stared down at her.

"You can't put yourself in dangerous situations like that. Oliver needs you."

"I didn't put myself in a dangerous situation. I refuse to take the blame for being in the wrong place at the wrong time. But what I did do is protect myself and possibly keep an already abused wife from being further abused."

She poked his arm once for good measure.

He had the good sense to look contrite. "You're right, I'm sorry. It worried me."

"It wasn't fun for me, either." She winced because everything hurt now.

Marcus sighed as he stared down at her and then, before she could brace herself or object, he scooped her up and held her as if she was a five-year-old child. She tried to get loose, but his arms tightened around her and she was forced close, feeling the strength in his arms.

Suddenly, objecting became the last thing she wanted to do as she settled in his arms and felt his warmth, felt the strong beat of his heart. As they went out the door, Pastor Matthews provided an umbrella, shoving it into her hands, and then he tossed her an already damp jacket. A jacket that smelled like Marcus.

"You all be careful out there," the pastor warned, and she wondered if the warning had a double meaning.

Marcus picked up his pace as they headed for his truck.

"I could walk," she offered.

"I know you can. But you look like you might collapse. You're not heavy."

"Thank you. I think."

A moment later they were at his truck, and he managed to pull the door open and deposit her in the seat without ever letting her feet touch the ground. She pulled on her seat belt as he went around to get in on the driver's side.

Not surprisingly, he climbed in without a word. In the dark interior of the truck, barely illuminated by the distant light at the front of the church and the orange glow of a streetlight, she saw the harsh set of his mouth. He was a thing of beauty, with chiseled features, a strong mouth and dark eyes.

If she didn't know better, she might think he was mad at her. But she did know better. She knew he was worried. Upset. *For her.*

He caught her staring and quirked a brow. As they pulled from the parking lot, he turned up the radio, a country station playing softly.

"Stop staring." He finally spoke, his voice soft and raspy.

"What happened?" She felt a strong pull toward him and a need to know his stories. It couldn't lead anywhere, this attraction or the other deeper, more startling emotions. Proof yet again that she had a radar for dark and brooding men.

But she wanted his stories.

"Happened?" He peered through the rain-splattered windshield as the wipers worked to keep it clear. The road was dark and the lines nearly invisible.

"Nothing, focus on the road."

They hit standing water and the truck hydroplaned, swerving just a bit. He grimaced and kept a tight hand on the wheel.

"Relax," he told her.

"What if the bridge is out?" she asked.

"You're all about the positive, aren't you?" He kept his attention on the road.

"Sorry."

He slowed as the rain came down harder. "My dad."

The two words spoken in his raspy voice took her by surprise. She shifted in the seat and studied his face, the clenched jaw, the way his hands gripped the wheel.

"Your dad?"

"You asked what happened. My dad did this to me. I was—" he shrugged "—I guess maybe fourteen. I don't remember. Must have been the lack of oxygen to my brain as he tried to choke the life out of me."

"Why?" The word came out as a whisper. Shock made her feel cold. She shivered in his jacket, which still covered her.

"Lucy and her husband, Dane. Back then they'd been sneaking around, dating. My dad didn't allow dating. When he found out, he ran Dane off and he locked Lucy in a storage room in the barn."

"You tried to get her out."

"Yeah. First Alex tried to talk to him. Alex is always the diplomat. When that didn't work, I tried to reason with him my way. I knocked him down and thought I'd take him with my fists. Unfortunately, he was bigger and stronger. Doc guesses he damaged my larynx. He also bashed my shin with a shovel. And left the scar on my face."

Tears fell. She brushed them away, but not before he saw.

"Don't," he warned. "I would do it again."

"I know you would."

"But I'm not a hero." He slowed the truck as they neared the turn to Essie's. "I'm a recovering alcoholic. I've never been good at being there for the people who needed me. I've let down more people than I can count."

She wanted to tell him he wasn't like his father. She wanted to assure him that she didn't believe he would ever harm his son. But what did she know about Marcus Palermo?

Nothing really.

She took that back. She knew that he was gentle with his son, cared about his family and was strong enough to carry her when she couldn't carry herself. She closed her eyes, remembering those moments in his arms. She'd felt safe.

He'd made her feel protected. More than once.

He'd also made her feel more. More unsure. More terrified of her own emotions. More drawn to him than she had ever been drawn to any man.

He parked under the portico at the side of Essie's house and told her to slide across and get out on the driver's side. She did, knowing this time he wouldn't carry her. He didn't even reach for her hand. Instead, he hurried up the steps and opened the door that led through the breakfast room.

"Are you hungry?" he asked as they entered the kitchen.

"A little."

He opened the fridge. "There's leftover potato soup."

She took the container from his hands. Strong hands. The thought unnerved her. She moved away from him, finding a bowl and then pulling out another for him. He didn't object, so she filled both bowls and heated them in the microwave.

They didn't sit down to eat. They stood side by side in the kitchen with just the light over the sink and the rain pouring down outside. Somewhere a clock ticked away the seconds. They were too close. The moment felt companionable and more. She avoided looking at him, afraid of what she would see in his eyes and afraid of what he would see in hers. She was afraid of him, but it wasn't the kind of fear that raised her hackles or made her worry for her safety.

Marcus finished his soup and poured two glasses of iced tea. He set hers on the counter behind her and carried his to the breakfast room, leaving her alone. After a few minutes she followed him, knowing he had walked away to be alone with his thoughts, with the past.

She had forced him to think back on the

abuse. Unsettled by that, she stepped close, needing to comfort him. He took a deep breath, and as she slid an arm around his waist, he stiffened. She wasn't going to let him get away with that. If he was going to be Oliver's dad, he needed to learn to embrace, to hug, to touch.

Little boys might be snips, snails and puppy dog tails, but they still needed warmth and they needed affection. Marcus had obviously gotten the short end of those two things as a child.

Slowly he moved until they were facing each other. He took a breath and relaxed, and she wrapped her arms tighter, holding him close. She wouldn't lie to herself and say this was her way of comforting a man who had been hurt. The man in her arms wasn't that child anymore. He leaned forward, touching his forehead to hers.

Rain trickled down the windows and thunder rumbled in the distance. Slowly the moment continued to shift and change until it became something that stole her breath. He moved and she looked up, searching his dark eyes as he changed position, lowering his mouth to capture hers.

Softly his lips brushed hers, the touch so light it almost didn't happen. She sighed into the kiss and then his lips met hers a little more insistently. A little more desperately.

Their hands remained intertwined. He pulled a hand loose to sweep it across her cheek, holding her there for the sweet exploration of his kiss. His touch was soft, gentle and sure.

Slowly he drew back, closing his eyes and murmuring her name. His fingers loosened and he let go of her hand.

"I have to go." He took a cautious step back. "I shouldn't have done that. I'm not going to do it again."

"No?" She disliked that it came out as a question. It should have been a definite no. They wouldn't do this again.

"My days of playing the field are over," he explained, answering the question that shouldn't have been a question. "And I'm the last thing you need in your life."

"Thank you for explaining that." She could have told him it was too late. Sammy had put them in each other's lives. For better or worse.

His mouth kicked up at the corner, and an almost amused look flickered through his eyes. "You're welcome."

And then he left. As a parting shot, she should have said something like *You got that right, buddy. You're the last thing I need in my life.*

Instead, she stood at the window watching him drive away and arguing all the reasons he was right and insisting her sanity had taken a momentary leave of absence. Tomorrow would be different. She'd be sane again. It wouldn't be dark and rainy. They wouldn't both be in this vulnerable place.

The connection would be broken, she assured herself. She sighed, her forehead pushed against the cool glass of the window as the rain continued to fall. It was dark. So dark out there in the country with no streetlights, no houses. She'd never felt so alone.

Maybe that was the place Marcus had touched tonight, her loneliness. Maybe they'd both been lonely and it had drawn them to each other.

Whatever. She could convince herself of anything, but the truth was she liked him. He wasn't at all the person she'd expected. And he was dangerous to her heart. Dangerous to her convictions.

Her first priority had to be Oliver. His future. His happiness and safety.

She'd spent her childhood being the victim of her single mother's poor choices. Oliver wasn't going to be the victim of her poor choices. Throughout her childhood, Lissa had been an afterthought. Her safety had been an afterthought. Her mother's relationships, the men, had come first.

As attractive as Marcus Palermo might be, Lissa wouldn't get sidetracked. Not when the man she found herself attracted to was the same man who could take Oliver from her.

Forever.

Chapter Ten

"Wake up. We've got to roll."

The words penetrated Marcus's sleep-fogged brain. He covered his head with a pillow. "Go away, Alex."

He brought his arm up and peeked at his watch. Five in the morning. His alarm would go off in an hour. Since he hadn't slept much last night, he wasn't even thinking about getting up an hour early with his brother, who obviously believed the saying about the early bird getting the worm.

"Out of bed."

"I don't like worms," Marcus muttered. "You go get all you want."

"Town's flooding, you slug. Get up. We have to get stuff out of the café before the creek reaches it."

That got his attention. "My house."

"Yeah, I know. If you hurry, we can make a loop and go by your place before we head to town." The door closed.

Marcus could still hear the rain. As he headed down the hall a few minutes later, he could also hear Marissa and Alex in the kitchen. They were whispering, and even without seeing, he knew they were cuddled up and talking all sweet to each other. He couldn't decide whether to be disgusted by the display or find it amusing and cute.

He was disgusted. That was what he decided when he walked into the kitchen and they were standing close, arms around each other.

"Too early in the morning to subject me to this." He poured himself a cup of coffee. "I thought we were in a hurry."

"We are in a hurry." Alex filled a thermos with coffee.

"We should check on Essie." Marcus sat down to pull on boots. When he looked up, Alex and Marissa were sharing a look. "Did I say something funny?"

"No, not at all." Smirking, Alex tossed him a granola bar. "Let's go."

Marcus headed out the door ahead of his brother, shrugging into a jacket as he went. He pushed his hat down on his head as he hurried across the yard to Alex's truck. It took his twin a few minutes longer, standing in the doorway of the house kissing his wife.

Jealousy. It came out of nowhere. Marcus had never been jealous of his brother. Well, maybe once or twice, when school had come easy to Alex. Or when he'd managed to talk his way through anger instead of fighting with their father. But when it came to women, no, he'd never been envious. The two of them wanted different things. Alex had a more settled personality. He wanted the minivan and family vacations.

Marcus had been telling himself for as long as he could remember that he didn't want those things. It was easier to shut himself off than to open up and be rejected. Or to open up and think about hurting someone.

When Alex finally climbed behind the wheel of the truck, Marcus had settled his emotions. He refilled his insulated mug with coffee from the thermos and gave a quick shake of his head at the silly grin on his brother's face.

"What?" Alex grinned because he knew. And he wasn't at all ashamed.

"I'm happy for you," Marcus admitted. He glanced out the window and sipped his coffee.

"Thanks, because I'm pretty happy for myself. We're having a baby."

Just like that, everything changed. The hot

coffee scalded when Marcus spilled it on his shirt. He sat up a little straighter and gave Alex a quick look to see if the expression on his face matched the tone.

"A baby." He laughed a little, thinking about his brother as a dad.

"Well, it isn't like you don't have one of your own."

That changed the mood in the truck. Oliver had been a baby. His baby. He hadn't known that a kid with his DNA was living on the same planet, breathing the same Texas air, learning to walk and talk. "Yeah, I do have a son of my own."

"It's a lot to take in, isn't it?"

"Yeah, it's a lot. But he's a good kid."

"So you'll keep him?"

"He's my son, Alex. Not a puppy I found on the side of the road." Marcus shot his brother a look. "Is there really a question about that? I don't know how I'm going to do this, but I can't imagine him not being here with us. We're his family."

"I know that. But a few days ago, I think you weren't as crazy about the idea. Also, there's Lissa to consider. He's been with her for a while."

"I know all of that."

"I never thought this would be our lives."

Alex turned onto the main road, but he kept the speed down and dodged standing water on the pavement. "We were all a pretty dysfunctional mess. But we've kind of pulled ourselves out of that pit."

Marcus shrugged it off. "Yeah, I guess we have. Thank God and Essie."

They pulled up to Essie's a few minutes later. Their aunt stood on the front porch with Lissa. The two were scanning the horizon, where there wasn't much to see but more clouds and more rain coming. Essie raised her coffee cup in greeting.

"Well?" she asked as they walked up the steps to the porch.

"We're heading to my place and then to town," Marcus said. "We thought we'd check on you all before we head that way."

"Check on me, my foot." Essie gave him a long look. "I don't guess you could load up an entire café in that truck of yours."

"I wish we could," Marcus replied. "But we can get anything out that you want."

"My pictures on the walls and the register. I guess that's about all we'll be able to take out. I'm hoping that even if the water gets up in the building, it won't take everything."

"We'll stack tables and chairs against the

far wall in the kitchen." Alex gave their aunt a quick hug. "And we'll say some prayers."

"More than that, we cannot do." Essie sighed. "I've been praying for a few days now, and it doesn't look like the good Lord is bringing this rain to a stop anytime soon. I know He could. And I know for some reason He isn't. But I also know we'll make it through this the way we've made it through everything else life has thrown at us."

There was a point to that little sermon. Marcus figured it had something to do with rain and prayer, and something to do with his life. Essie pursed her lips and gave him that dead-on serious look of hers. Yeah, the message was for him. He'd make it through this. The way he'd made it through so many things. Actually, when it came right down to it, finding out he had a son wasn't such a bad thing after all.

As if on cue, the door opened and Oliver hurried out to join them. He saw Marcus and a big grin split his face. A moment later arms were wrapped around his waist.

Marcus patted the boy on the back and then made unfortunate eye contact with Lissa. Her look prodded him to give more of himself. He hugged his son to him and then scooped him up in his arms.

"What are you doing up this early?" Marcus asked Oliver.

"I heard Lissa and Aunt Essie talking." Marcus guessed his shock must have shown on his face. "She said I can call her Aunt Essie because she's an aunt and I need another aunt."

"That makes good sense," Marcus agreed.

Oliver wiggled to get down and Marcus put him back on his feet. "Aunt Essie said she can't open the café today. Because of flooding. But she's going to make pancakes. She said pancakes were always your favorite. They're mine, too. That must be because we have the same last name. Marcus Palermo and Oliver Palermo. I think that's cool."

"Yeah, that is cool." Marcus had to agree. Who wouldn't?

He met Lissa's gaze over the top of her coffee cup as she took a sip. Why hadn't he thought about Oliver's last name? He had just assumed Sammy had given him her last name. But standing there in front of him, as proud as he could be, was Marcus's flesh and blood. And he had his last name.

He'd gone through times in life when he hadn't been too proud of the name. He had thought about changing it so he wouldn't have that connection with his father. But now, Oliver having his last name changed everything.

The last thing he wanted was for his son to be ashamed of who he was. He also didn't want Oliver to ever be ashamed to have him for a father.

"We should get started." Alex gave Marcus a nudge with his elbow. "I know you want to get down to your place, but we might not be able to make it over the low-water bridge that crosses the dry creek."

"Yeah, I was thinking the same. We do need to be heading on to town. We can do more good there than at my place." Marcus put a hand on Oliver's shoulder. "Take care of the ladies, okay?"

"I thought I would go with you. I might be able to help." Lissa, he realized, had on rubber boots and a raincoat.

"I don't think so," Marcus started. She froze him with those blue eyes of hers.

"I make my own decisions, Marcus."

Okay, he got it. She didn't want him to kiss her one night and tell her what to do the next. But the anger. He didn't get that.

He put his hands up in surrender. "Fine. Do you want us to take you to the clinic? I'm assuming Oliver is staying with Essie?"

"Yes, Oliver is staying with me," Essie responded as she placed a hand on his son's shoulder. "I am leaving the search and rescue to you younger folk."

"Yes, you can drop me at the clinic at the shelter." Lissa was coming down the stairs. "I want to help Doc. And I want to be there with Pearl. They are still searching for her mother."

"Hold down the fort, Oliver." Marcus touched his son's shoulder. They had to tell him—soon, when things calmed down and they could spend time talking things out.

"I will. I'm pretty good at that. I build forts at Grammy Jane's house."

"I bet you are." He grinned at the boy's exuberance.

Oliver pointed at him, a huge smile flashing across his little face. "I made you smile. Aunt Essie said you almost never laugh. Everyone laughs. Don't they, Marcus?"

Marcus shot his aunt a look. They ought to be more careful what they say, because Oliver was obviously pretty good at eavesdropping.

"Yeah, everyone laughs." Marcus ruffled his son's hair. "Go on inside and enjoy those pancakes. Make sure you get bacon."

"Knock knock." Oliver looked up at him, waiting.

"What?"

"Knock knock. You're supposed to say 'who's there?'"

"Am I really?" Marcus blinked, confused by the way the conversation had turned.

"Say it so we can leave," Alex prodded.

"Who's there?" Marcus asked.

"Atch."

"Atch who?"

"Gesund…" Oliver bit down on his bottom lip. *"Gesundhigh."*

Marcus didn't crack a smile, but he wanted to. "Nope."

"It was a joke," Oliver told him.

"Gotta go." Marcus headed down the steps with Alex chuckling behind him.

"That kid is going to get the best of you." Alex spoke as they were driving toward Blue-bonnet.

"He *is* the best of me." Marcus didn't mean to be emotional about it, but he was late to the fatherhood party. He'd ridden some bulls, made some money, bought the farm he'd always wanted. But the kid, he was everything and then some.

He'd forgotten Lissa. She hurried after them, grabbing the door when he started to get in. He moved back and motioned her inside the cab of the truck.

"You're sure you want to skip your place?" Alex asked as they headed down the road.

"I moved what was important. And the stuff upstairs should be safe."

"Paintings," Alex told Lissa. He ignored Marcus's warning look. "You saw the ones downstairs, right?"

"Yes, I did. They're very good." Lissa gave Marcus a questioning look, and he didn't feel inclined to give answers.

Alex didn't stop. "Marcus is an artist."

"Okay, end of discussion. That's private."

"He sells them at a store in San Antonio. On the River Walk." Alex grinned, enjoying himself a little too much.

Marcus turned his attention to the window. Forget it. He wasn't winning this one.

Her phone rang. Marcus watched as she glanced at the caller ID.

"Block the caller."

She looked up. "What?"

"Same caller you've been ignoring for a week now. Block it if you don't want to talk."

"I'm not answering because he wanted to give me his opinion and try to control my days, my time and my life."

She couldn't be any clearer than that. It wasn't his business. One kiss didn't give him the right to tell her what to do. He got it.

"Your life. I'm not telling you what to do."

She dropped the phone back in her purse. "If I block him, I won't know what he's up to."

That got his attention. "Are you afraid of him, Lissa?"

"Not afraid. As you know, I can take care of myself. But he does make me nervous. He has met me in the parking garage of the hospital. He says he's there to make sure I get safely to my car."

"Have Security take you to your car. I'm not making that an order, just a friendly suggestion."

And now he wanted to pound this guy. A man he didn't know. A man he would never meet. But a man who made her expression tight with fear, even if she didn't call it fear. So much for not getting involved. Without trying, she'd pulled him into her life and made him care.

They turned into the church parking lot and the conversation ceased. He willingly let it go. It wasn't his business. She wasn't his business.

An ambulance pulled in behind them. That got all of their attention. The attendants climbed out the back. As they did, Marcus noticed a woman emerging. She was wrapped in blankets, and her hair was soaked and hanging around her pale face.

"Pearl's mommy," Lissa whispered, her

voice wobbly with emotion. "Please God, let that be Pearl's mom."

They got out as Pastor Matthews was running toward the ambulance. The woman sobbed, falling into his arms. They could hear him telling her she had saved her daughter.

Lissa's hand slid into Marcus's, the most natural gesture in the world. He gave her slim fingers a slight squeeze and she leaned into his shoulder, surrounding him with her warmth.

"There's your answer." He whispered the words against her hair and then, carefully, he kissed the top of her head.

"Yes, there's the answer." She smiled up at him. "You guys go rescue the world. I'll be here with Doc."

They watched the reunion between Pearl and her mother, and then they left. As they drove through town, Alex and Marcus were both shocked. The water had come up over the tracks and was rushing along the side of the café. It wasn't inside the building, but it was close. "Let's make a sweep through town before we tackle the café," Marcus suggested. "I'll check the state website and see if they have changed the projected cresting of the creek. If they haven't, the water probably won't get in the café."

"I think the rain is supposed to move out of

the area later this afternoon," Alex answered. "But I'm afraid that isn't going to do us a lot of good." They drove down a side road lined with houses. The waters from the creek had become a river, rushing out of the banks and sweeping through houses that were a good hundred feet from the banks of the normally shallow creek.

"Is that Dan Godfrey on his front porch?" Marcus asked as they drove along the street above where the flooded creek had overtaken the houses and the road that ran parallel to the water.

About a half block ahead of them Marcus could see the elderly man standing on his porch, his pants rolled up to his knobby knees. He had a big box in his skinny arms and a cat sitting on the box.

"What in the world?" Alex hit the brakes and pulled his truck to the side of the road. "How did search and rescue miss him? I heard they rescued Chet Wilkins and that crazy pig of his. The two were sitting in a canoe next to Chet's house."

"If I know Dan, he probably didn't answer the door. Or he hid, thinking he's lived there his whole life and that creek has never gotten close to his house."

"Yeah, there's a big X on his door, so they

did check the house. And you're right, he probably hid."

The two of them got out and headed in the direction of Dan's house. Alex yelled, telling the older man to stay put. The waters were rushing, and no way could Dan stand up against that current.

"Do you think we can get to him?" Marcus asked as they neared the house. The water was already to his knees and it would be deeper when they got to the front porch.

"I think we can stand up against the water. I like that Dan has his pants rolled up to his knees. The water is probably up to his waist."

"I'll carry Dan if you grab the box and the cat," Marcus offered.

"You hate cats so much you're willing to take the old man?"

Marcus grinned at that. "Yep."

The current pushed against them as they walked. All the time, Dan remained on the porch with his box and the cat. Water rushed around his house and was already several inches over the porch where he stood.

"Time to get you out of here, Dan." Alex took the box and the cat.

"I didn't want to leave Annie's house." The old man swiped at a tear as he mentioned his wife. "She loved this place. I had to get her doilies and the pictures of the kids. And this old cat."

"Did search and rescue let you stay?" Marcus asked.

Dan shook his head, his gray eyes faded and sad. "No, I climbed up in the attic when they came. I guess they thought I left with Billy. But Billy couldn't find me, either."

Billy was Dan's son. He lived in Killeen and got back as often as possible to see his dad.

"Is there anything else you want out of here, Dan?" Alex offered.

"No, I've got my memories. Sixty years' worth. Annie and I built this house the year we married. Back then there was money working in the oil fields." The older man looked at his house, all the emotion visible in his expression. "We had a good life here, me and Annie. Raised four kids. Had a passel of grands."

"You'll be able to come back," Alex assured him.

"No, I don't think Billy will let me. I heard him tell his wife that I'm slipping. I ain't, but that's what they think. After this they'll probably move me to the city and one of them homes."

Marcus felt for the man. He couldn't imagine leaving the place he'd built and lived in for sixty years. It was hard enough envisioning losing the home he'd had for less than a year. A home with memories built through another family, not his own.

"Maybe he'll let you stay in town, Dan." Marcus offered. "But we can't stay here right now. The water is seeping into the house and it's still coming up."

"I guess we'd better go." Dan sighed as he looked at the swollen creek. "I didn't think it would get like this. I thought a few inches, and if it came up, I'd just walk out. I didn't even move my old Ford out of the carport. I guess I won't have a truck after this."

Sure enough, water was pouring through Dan's old truck.

"It looks like you'll have to say goodbye to that truck." Alex held on to the cat and Marcus bit back a smile. That cat was going to have to ride in his brother's truck.

"Come on, Dan, time to go." Marcus scooped Dan up, and the older man kicked a little.

"I ain't no silly woman needing you to carry me out of here, Marcus Palermo."

"I know you're not, Dan. But that water is strong and you don't weigh much."

"I can walk out of here," Dan insisted in a

stronger voice than he'd used in a while. Marcus set him on his own two feet. "I don't mind if you hold me steady, but I'll not have you carrying me. What would Annie think if she was here?"

Marcus didn't argue. A man had his pride. "Come on, then."

Slowly they trudged back through the water. Dan had a hard time staying on his feet, but Marcus kept hold of him. He understood that the older man wanted to preserve his dignity. Marcus would help him do that. Besides, at least Marcus didn't have to hold on to that screaming, yowling cat.

The house Marcus grew up in was a sprawling, single-story ranch house. The stable and arena were several hundred feet from the house. Lissa walked through the stable with Oliver. Lucy had picked up Essie and Oliver and driven to the church to get Lissa. The guys were still busy in town helping people save what could be saved and rescuing those who hadn't gotten out in time.

Ahead of them, Marissa Palermo talked about the horses her husband, Alex, raised and the cattle. He also had bucking bulls.

Marissa taught at the local school, but school had let out for summer break. As she talked,

Marissa touched her belly. Often. If Lissa had to guess, she would say that other woman was pregnant.

"Can I ride a horse?" Oliver hurried ahead of them and stopped at a stall door where a big, gray head stretched over the door, eager for attention. The horse lipped at Oliver's hair and then blew out a breath. Oliver laughed and backed away, but then he inched forward again, raising a hand to pet the same velvety nose that had snorted on him.

"I think maybe when the rain stops we can arrange that." Marissa stood next to Oliver, her hand going again to her belly. "This is Granite. He's Alex's favorite."

"I like him, too." Oliver smiled up at her.

She was his aunt. Lissa realized that as she watched the two, Alex and Marissa. Oliver had no idea that he was surrounded by aunts, uncles and cousins. Marcus was right—they needed to tell him as soon as possible. Oliver deserved to know these people and to know they were his family.

The more time she spent with them, the less she worried about Oliver's future. He would have these people in his life. The more she got to know them, though, the more she felt her heart ache with loss that was eminent.

Oliver spotted a cat and took off, eager to catch it.

"Be careful, some of these cats are a little wild," Marissa cautioned. "But if you look around, you might find kittens. Just don't go in stalls with horses."

When he heard the word *kittens*, Oliver slowed his pace and started a search. Marissa sat down on the bench placed midway along the aisle. Lissa sat with her.

"How far along are you?" Lissa asked.

At the question, Marissa smiled a sweet smile. "Just a few months. We haven't told anyone."

"I think you'll have to tell them soon," Lissa advised. "You're glowing."

At that, Marissa turned a shade of pink and her hand went to her belly again. "We're just so excited. It's twins. They did an ultrasound last week and there are two little Palermos on the way."

"Wow! That's exciting."

"And frightening," Marissa added. She watched as Oliver crawled under the door of a stall.

Lissa checked to make sure it was empty and then sat back, relaxing. The rain had slowed and was now a gentle patter on the metal roof of the stable.

"I watch him and I think, I'm going to have one like him. He's so stinking cute that I just can't wait." Marissa glanced at Lissa. "They'll be cousins."

Lissa nodded, keeping an eye on Oliver as he continued the search for kittens. At one time Marcus would have been a child living here, playing in this barn. No, she rethought that. Did he ever play? Did the Palermo children have happy memories? It would be a shame if they didn't have those good memories, having grown up in a place like this, with so much to offer.

Oliver continued his search through the barn. He stopped at a closed door and peeked at Lissa before turning the handle and slowly pulling the door open.

"I should check on him." She stood. "He's not been himself since we picked him up earlier. He might be getting homesick."

Marissa touched her arm. "Don't let him play in that room. Marcus wouldn't want him in there."

"No?"

"It's a difficult story and not mine to tell."

"Of course. I'll go get him."

Maria entered the barn as Lissa hurried to collect Oliver. The younger Palermo smiled a greeting before nodding toward the room Oliver had entered.

"Better get him out of there," Maria warned. "Marcus and Alex just pulled up."

Oliver, being five, didn't understand the meaning of *hurry*. He had found a litter of kittens. The mama cat curled around them, licking them in turns and nuzzling them as they curled against her belly.

"Can I take one home with me?" Oliver asked as Lissa squatted next to him.

"No, we can't have cats in our apartment. Remember?"

Oliver looked crestfallen at the reminder. "Yeah, I know. I like it here. There are cats and dogs and horses."

"Yes, there are. But we don't live in the country."

"No, we live in a big, big city." Oliver ran a finger over a little striped tabby kitten. "I like this one."

"He is pretty," Lissa agreed. "We need to go now."

"What have you all found?"

The soft but gruff voice startled Lissa. She jumped a little and faced the door, feeling guilty for having been caught in the room that Marcus wouldn't want her in.

He didn't look upset. His expression softened as he looked from her to Oliver. His son had worked up the courage to pick up the tabby kitten.

"Kittens, huh?" Marcus remained at the door.

"Come in and see them. There are six." Oliver kissed the kitten on the top of the head. "How does the mom get to them when the door is closed?"

"She goes up in the loft and comes down. See the little opening?" Marcus pointed at the ceiling, and sure enough the wall didn't go to the top. There was a ledge and an opening that led to the loft. It was only about six inches wide, but big enough for a cat.

"I want a kitten, but we can't have cats in the city," Oliver informed Marcus with a glum expression on his face.

"Oliver, you should put the kitten back with his mommy. She's looking for him." Lissa stroked the kitten's soft head, and then she helped Oliver return him to the mother cat.

"Have you seen the kittens?" Oliver asked, unaware of how Marcus seemed frozen at the door of the room. "You should see them. They're all colors."

"I bet they're pretty. And if you didn't live in the city, you could take one home with you."

Marcus looked from Oliver to Lissa and she wanted to tell him that was unfair.

"Yeah, but we can't live in the country. Lissa has a job in San Antonio. And she doesn't really think she could work for Doc Parker. We just came here so I could meet you." Did his voice seem off? Upset? Lissa heard it, but she wanted to believe she didn't.

"You have been eavesdropping again," Marcus said quietly, as was his way.

"I hear a lot of stuff," Oliver said, not bothering to look up. His attention remained on the cats. "I know that Marcus is my dad. That's why I have his last name. And I'm the spitting image of him. Whatever that is."

"Spitting image," Lissa whispered, her throat clogged with emotions that felt like sadness, regret and loss. She was going to lose Oliver to this place and these people. They were his family, she reminded herself, and she had no claim to him. The letter gave Marcus the rights. The right to choose Oliver. The right to keep him from her.

Marcus was at her side. She hadn't noticed him moving into the room. She felt his hand on her shoulder, and then he squatted next to her, his hand sliding down her arm and then away.

"You are my spitting image," he told Oliver

in his quiet voice. "But you're a far sight better than me."

"My mom said I had a dad and that I couldn't meet him because he would take me and he wasn't no good." Oliver looked him over and his mouth drew into a frown. "I guess she meant you."

Lissa's heart shattered. Sammy never should have told Oliver those things. Why would she do that to him? She sighed because she knew. Sammy hadn't always thought about Oliver's feelings.

Marcus sat on the floor, moving so that his back was against the wall. He pulled Oliver onto his lap. "I'm really sorry your mom told you that. And I wish I had known you a lot sooner so we could work up to this whole father-and-son thing."

"Because you're sorry that you didn't want to be around me?"

Lissa looked at Marcus, unsure of what answer he would or should give a five-year-old child. His eyes reflected her surprise. Leave it to Oliver to ask the hard questions.

"I've made a lot of mistakes and I'm trying to make up for those mistakes. Oliver, I am very sorry that I didn't get to be around you."

He didn't say anything against Sammy, who hadn't told him he had a son. Lissa mouthed a silent *Thank you.* He nodded and continued to talk to his son in a quiet and comforting tone.

"Will I live here now? Instead of with Lissa? My bed is at her house. And I have a bed at Grammy and Pops's. We always lived with Lissa, though." His little face fell as he looked from one adult to the other.

Lissa felt the ache of loss as never before. She'd been holding this little boy since he took his first breath. She'd changed his diapers. She'd helped Sammy potty train him. She'd taught him the alphabet and his colors.

Marcus's gaze bored into her, questioning her without words. Oliver had revealed so much. More than she'd been willing to tell.

Oliver crawled off his lap. "You just don't want to be a dad. That's what I heard them say in town."

Marcus paled beneath the accusation. He opened his mouth. Lissa waited, wanting him to say the right thing. But what could he say to that. He had never planned on being a dad. He didn't trust himself to be a dad.

"It's something I have to get used to, Oliver." He stood, his hand going to the boy's. "I haven't been a dad before."

He looked to Lissa, clearly lost and unsure of how to handle the hurt his son was experiencing.

"Oliver, we'll talk about this. Maybe it's nap time?" Lissa reached for his hand.

Oliver ran out of the storage room and into the waiting arms of Maria. His aunt Maria, Lissa realized.

"I don't want a nap," Oliver responded, burying his face against Maria as her arms went around him. "I want my mommy."

Tears trickled down Maria's cheeks as she soothed the little boy. "How about we go to the house and have cookies and milk? I'll put in a movie and we'll cuddle."

Lissa ached to hold him, to comfort him. She had been prepared to lose him, or so she'd thought. Bringing him here, she'd known she was giving him up to Marcus. But she hadn't expected to feel this distance as Oliver picked someone else's arms over hers.

A strong arm went around her waist, offering comfort. She nodded and told Maria that sounded like a great idea. The younger woman lifted Oliver and carried him from the stable. Marissa had also left, which meant she and Marcus were alone.

And then she was in his arms and he was holding her as she cried against his shoulder. His lips touched her hair and he murmured that it would work out. They would figure this out and do what was best for Oliver.

His next words were ones she wasn't prepared for. "You have to tell me more about Sammy. Oliver was living with you. There has to be a reason for that."

She nodded, admitting that there had been a reason. She had hoped she wouldn't have to discuss the mess her best friend and foster sister had made of parenting.

Worse, the feeling that she was closer than ever to losing Oliver. And the man holding her, offering her comfort, was the man who would take him from her.

Chapter Eleven

"Let's take a ride to my place," Marcus told the woman he'd carefully set aside after hugging her through the worst of her tears. She brushed a hand across her face and drew in a deep breath.

"I guess we should talk."

Not that long ago Pastor Matthews had told him that the closer he got to God, the more his faith would be tested. He'd never been too good at tests. This time he couldn't fail. There was too much riding on his choices and the outcome.

How in the world did he part Lissa from Oliver? Worse, he couldn't let his son go. A week changed everything, it seemed. God created the heavens and the earth in six days. And in about the same amount of time He'd turned

Marcus into a father. A man who couldn't begin to think of signing away his rights.

"We can drive over to my place. I need to check on things there."

She nodded and followed him out of the barn. The rain had stopped. Alex emerged from the tractor-repair shop he'd built on the property and saw them heading toward the old farm truck. He stepped back inside the garage and came out with keys.

"You might need these."

"Thanks. Don't send out a posse. We might be a while."

"Marcus," Alex warned.

Marcus raised a hand to wave him away. "I'm fine."

He wasn't going to lose his temper. He wasn't even thinking of taking a drink. At least he had that going for him. He just wanted to know everything. And the only one who could tell him the entire story was the woman walking next to him, acting as if she was on her way to walk the plank.

"I'm fine," he repeated, this time for her benefit.

He opened the door and she climbed in the truck. Blue eyes locked with his. He reached to touch her pale cheek. Her eyes closed beneath his touch, but she moved closer, curving into his palm in the sweetest way.

He felt as if she'd turned him inside out and upside down. He didn't know front from back, right from left. Somehow he had to find his old, steady self, the man who kept emotion on the back burner. Cold-as-Ice Palermo, they'd called him. That had been a million years ago, it seemed.

He closed the door and walked to the driver's side of the truck. When he got in, he turned the radio to a cowboy country station that he liked. Soulful lyrics about open roads, rodeo, sweethearts and gentle rains. All the things a man could dream about but never thought could be reality.

"She slipped," Lissa said as they drove.

Tires hummed on the drying pavement. In the west there was a flash of red through gray clouds as the sun set on the horizon.

"Slipped?"

"After she had Oliver. She stopped working. She went out with a guy. She started drinking. You have to understand, she told me that she'd broken up with you because you were angry and wild, drank too much and she was afraid of you. That's the excuse she gave for not telling you about Oliver."

"I'm a mean drunk?" He said the words, not

quite understanding. "That's why I didn't get to see my son until he was five years old? And you kept him from me an extra year."

He fought down the anger. But he had to be fair. It wasn't really Lissa he was angry with. He noticed the fear in her blue eyes. He didn't want her afraid of him. He wanted her trust. That made this about the most complicated relationship of his life.

But it wasn't a relationship. They shared one thing, Oliver. Maybe they shared a friendship. And now he realized they shared distrust.

"I knew you would take him from me. The letter gives you the right."

"You're right, it does. And I will." He couldn't begin to explain how it felt to know what was taken from him, with no thought to his feelings or Oliver's. He was going to make it right.

"I know."

"You're the one who raised him." He watched as tears gathered in her eyes and she nodded. "Not Sammy?"

It was the story of the two women in Solomon's court. The one said to split the baby in half. The true mother was willing to spare her child and give him up.

No matter what, Oliver would be split. His

anger with her lessened to a slow simmer. "We'll figure something out."

"Figure something out?"

"Some way to share custody. You could take that job Doc offered. It would be easier for him to split his time between us." He had other reasons for that suggestion. It would make it easier for Marcus to see her. If he kept her near, he would see her, hear her laugh, share Oliver's big adventures as he grew up.

"I can't. I have a job. I have an apartment."

"Okay. Well, we'll have to give this time and work on something that is good for Oliver."

"For what it's worth, I'm sorry."

He sighed. "Yeah, me too. And for what it's worth... I don't blame you. I just don't want to give up my son."

"I know."

Yeah, she knew. Because she considered Oliver her son, too. He might not lose his temper, but it would have felt good to hit something.

They pulled down the road to his place. With the windows down, he could hear the water roaring.

Slowing to a stop, he sat in his truck and stared at the old farmhouse that he'd planned to spend his life in. He had known it would need work. He'd planned on reinforcing the porch and putting in new windows. It was hard to take it all in, the collapsed porch roof, the broken windows. The tree that had fallen, crashing into the roof.

He got out and headed toward the back door. It took a hard shove to get it open. And then it took a full minute to get his bearings.

As he'd expected, the floodwaters had receded and left behind mud and silt, leaves and small branches that had come through the broken windows. A yowling sound, faint but miserable, echoed from the rafters. He stepped back into the living room and listened, waiting to see where the sound came from. When he heard it again, he followed it to the spare bedroom. He peeked in the closet and saw golden eyes glowing from the shelf. The cat hissed.

"I'm thinking about helping you out of this situation if you calm down. But I'm not interested in getting clawed up."

He pulled off his jacket and reached for the loose skin on the back of the cat's neck. As soon as he had hold of the hissing feline, he wrapped it in his jacket. The cat fought a good fight but then settled in his arms.

"I'm not fond of cats."

"Yet here you are rescuing him." He spun to face Lissa. She stood in the doorway, humor shining from blue eyes that he thought he'd see in his dreams for the rest of his solitary life. If he ever allowed himself to dream of forever with someone, she'd look a lot like this woman.

Someday she'd be married to a doctor, maybe a business owner. They'd have some cute little kids. She'd have a good, stable life. The kind of life she probably dreamed about when she was a kid. The kind of life that would make her feel secure. And where would Oliver be? He noticed the cat had started to purr. Its wet fur had soaked his jacket and the T-shirt he wore. It didn't matter, because the only thing he could think of was what the future might hold for Oliver, and for him.

"You okay?" Lissa asked.

"Yeah, I'm fine. Not sure the same can be said for this trespasser that I found in my spare bedroom. I'd say he got caught in the creek and somehow he managed to get inside the closet and on the shelf."

"Brave cat. What about you, though? This is a lot to take in." She glanced around, making her point. His house, his dream, appeared to be trashed.

He shrugged it off as if it didn't matter. They both knew it did. It had been about more than a house, a building; it had been a legacy and feelings he'd had for a family that had shown him love.

This home had made him feel safe. In a tumultuous childhood, it had been his haven. But now, as he looked around, it looked as if the dream ended here, with the flood and devastation.

"You have insurance? You can rebuild."

Right. She made it sound easy, but a person couldn't rebuild memories. As wrong as it might sound to others, he couldn't imagine another house on this land. A new home would be an empty shell without memories of the family that had meant so much to him.

"Yes, I can rebuild." He gave her the answer she wanted to hear.

"What are you going to do with that cat?" she asked as they stood there in the kitchen.

He opened the fridge and found lunch meat. He opened the package and put it on the counter. The cat scrambled out of his jacket and attacked the meat, alternately growling and purring.

"I guess I'm going to feed it. And then name it. Lately, it seems as if animals and people find me."

"Yes, you've had your share of surprises. I guess a cat doesn't seem like a big deal after having a boy dropped on your doorstep."

She reached to pet the cat. It hissed but kept eating, allowing her to stroke its still damp fur.

Marcus leaned against the counter. "I've had

to do more self-examination in the last two weeks than I've done in my life. When you first showed up, being a dad was the furthest thing from my mind. I couldn't imagine letting a kid into my life. And now I can't imagine life without him." He glanced around the muddy kitchen and sighed. "But I also have a whole new set of concerns. What kind of life can I give him? I'm a single man without a real home."

Her hands touched his shoulders. He flinched when she traced a finger down the scar on his face. No one ever touched that scar.

"I didn't come here expecting you to be a person I would trust Oliver to. But I do. You're not the only one who has had to realize some cold, hard truths." She kissed his cheek. "You're good. And kind. Oliver needs you."

"But that would mean taking him from you."

"I know." And she backed away, hurt by his words.

"Like I said before, we'll figure something out," Marcus reassured her.

He headed up the stairs. Lissa followed. As they made the turn at the landing, the cat ran past them. He guessed the animal had decided to stay. He should probably name it. And buy some cat food.

Whatever thoughts he had on the cat, it didn't matter once they hit the upstairs bedroom.

"What in the world?" Lissa stepped inside the room, spinning to take it in.

"You did this?" she asked. But it was more of a statement.

"Yeah."

She touched a canvas with a painting of an abandoned church he'd seen while driving through the country. He'd had to tramp through a field of bluebonnets to take a picture. The old building had been surrounded by evergreens and barely visible from the road.

"Amazing."

"I enjoy it." It had been his therapy for years. "Some people journal their feelings. I used to sketch. And when I got a little money, I bought paints. The last few years of bull riding, as I was getting sober, the other guys would go to the bar."

"You'd stay in your room and paint."

"Bingo."

She reached for his hand. The gesture didn't make him feel trapped, but it did something to his heart he hadn't quite expected.

Lissa realized the moment she took hold of Marcus's hand that in the short time they'd known each other, she'd become comfortable with him. The small gestures such as holding his hand, kissing his cheek, seemed natural. It felt as if they had always been.

But she knew better than to let those feelings control her logical self. She'd learned that while working in the emergency room. The first time she'd had to treat an injured child and her emotions had almost clouded her judgment, she had realized that to be effective she had to put aside some of that emotion and keep her thinking clear.

The situation with Marcus was proving to be very similar. It would be easy to be drawn to him, to feel something for him. But clear thinking had to prevail.

As if reading her thoughts, he pulled his hand from hers and started moving paintings. He had a half-finished sketch of a horse standing in a field. She watched as he moved the canvas and others, stacking them neatly against the wall.

"What are you going to do with them?" she asked.

"Box them up and move them to Alex's. I'm afraid of the structure of this house. We probably shouldn't even be in here. It makes sense to get things out while I can."

With that he grabbed several of his paintings

and headed down the stairs with them. She picked up a couple more and followed. Voices carried, a child's higher tones, someone older, responding. As they entered the kitchen, the back door flew open and Oliver ran through, Alex behind him.

"Hey, we thought we'd come help." Alex pulled on leather gloves as he looked around. "This place is a disaster."

"Thanks." Marcus headed for the door, but then he paused, as if remembering something. He shifted the paintings and glanced back at Oliver. "Want to help me out, little man?"

With a quick nod, Oliver slid through the door and held it open for Marcus. And then the two of them were crossing the mud-soaked yard. Lissa watched from the window. She had placed the paintings she carried on the dining room table, leaving them for Marcus to retrieve. It was better this way, better if she gave Marcus and Oliver time alone, time to bond.

She needed time and distance, too. To let her heart get used to losing Oliver. Her gaze slid to the tall, handsome man walking next to the little boy. Her heart would miss him, too. That was an unexpected outcome of this trip and the two weeks she'd spent in Bluebonnet. The small town had grown on her. The man

Sammy had labeled dysfunctional had grown on her, as well.

As a friend. Just a friend. She wouldn't let him be more. Not that he wanted more. Not with her. They were too similar and, at the same time, too different.

"This is a real mess," Alex grumbled as he walked around the house.

"He doesn't think he can repair it."

Alex stepped back into the kitchen, where she still stood watching Marcus and Oliver as they loaded up the truck. Oliver said something and Marcus gave him a serious look.

"I wasn't talking about the house. He can build a new one."

"He doesn't want a new one. This house means something to him."

"I know. He used to sneak off and come over here. But anyway, I was referring to the situation with Marcus and Oliver. And you."

"It isn't a mess. It's life. Life is always messy."

"Yeah, and complicated."

Right, *complicated.*

Marcus and Oliver seemed to have forgotten the artwork. They were heading toward the barn. She stood for a few minutes watching as the two of them talked and then disappeared through the open double doors.

"You can go on out there," Alex said as he picked up the paintings she'd left on the table. "I'm going to load some of this up for him and then I'm heading back to my place to feed livestock. Tell Marcus that later I'll be in town to help some of the church members start the cleanup process."

"I'll let him know."

Alex patted her on the back and then he left. The gesture had been awkward but comforting. She smiled at the thought. Alex was a good brother. Marcus had a big support system to get him through this.

She wasn't so sure about herself. She didn't know who she would be without Oliver. She also knew she couldn't fight Marcus. She didn't have the money. And it wouldn't be right. Marcus was his biological parent.

Sighing, she started across the wide expanse of yard. From the barn she heard laughter. Oliver said something she couldn't quite hear and then he laughed again. She entered the dimly lit interior of the barn and saw the two of them working with a lasso. Marcus guided Oliver's hand as the little boy held the rope. Together they brought it up, circled it a few times and then let loose. The rope flew through the air, landing on horns stuck in a bale of hay.

"You almost got it that time," Marcus assured his son.

Oliver looked up at him, his face hidden beneath Marcus's hat. "I'm going to be a cowboy."

"Are you now?" Marcus asked. "There's a lot of other things you can be. A doctor or lawyer, maybe a policeman, or even a teacher."

"Yeah, but you're a cowboy and I'm your son."

Marcus put a hand on Oliver's shoulder. "Yeah, you are."

They were working it out. Oliver's anger that they'd hid his parentage from him. Marcus's lack of trust in himself. She didn't know where that left her. Alone, she guessed. No, not alone. She would still see Oliver. She had her parents, friends, coworkers.

She had a job offer to come here. But if she did, would that make things difficult for Oliver and Marcus? Would it complicate their ability to bond? She didn't want to do that to them.

Marcus noticed her first. He nodded his head in greeting, and when he did, Oliver looked up and noticed her. A grin spread across his face and he held up the rope as if it were a prize he'd won.

"Look, Lissa. I can rope! It isn't easy, but I did a good job."

"I saw that. I'm really proud of you." She reached to pet Marcus's dog. The animal plopped to its belly, sighing as he rested his head on his front paws. "Alex went home to feed his animals and then he's going to town to help with cleanup."

Marcus nodded. "I'm going to get what I can out of this place, and tomorrow see what I can do in town."

"How will people rebuild or replace what they've lost if they don't have flood insurance?"

"They will get help from government agencies. Some probably do have insurance to cover the damage, or at least the contents of their homes. And a lot of folks will just dig in, recoup what they can and make do."

"Maybe we can find a way to help?"

Marcus had a wheelbarrow and he tossed a couple of bags of feed in it. "We? As in you and me, or do you have a pet in your pocket I don't know about?"

"I wouldn't mind helping out."

"It takes time to put together a fund-raiser."

Meaning she'd be gone. Maybe he was right. Why would she even consider volunteering herself for something that would take weeks to pull off? By the time they could get it arranged, she'd be in San Antonio and back at work. She didn't even know what it was she wanted to arrange. She just wanted to help the small town that had become a big part of her life in a short amount of time.

"It'll work out," Marcus said quietly. "And if you want to tell Essie your idea, I'm sure she'd dig in and get it done."

They walked out the back door of the barn, Marcus pushing the wheelbarrow. He had explained that he had to feed his cattle but didn't want to get his truck stuck. He'd considered using his ATV, but then he'd have to get it from the equipment shed.

Oliver had run ahead of them. He returned, grinning big.

"Knock knock."

Marcus groaned. "Another one?"

Oliver nodded, walking backward to face them. "Yep."

"Who's there?" Marcus asked.

"Partridge." Oliver giggled as he said it.

"Partridge who?"

"Partridge who ate a pear tree."

"Nope." Marcus shook his head.

"Really?" Lissa asked. "You're not going to laugh?"

"He's going to have to do better than that." Marcus answered, but she saw the twinkle of amusement in his dark eyes.

He was enjoying this game of Oliver making up jokes to crack his seriousness. She guessed Oliver probably enjoyed it, too. It was a way for the two of them to bond.

"You're getting the hang of this parenting thing." She gave the compliment, meaning it. She knew what it meant for her, that he would soon take her place in Oliver's life. But he was the parent, not her, she reminded herself.

They continued on through the soggy grass, the wheelbarrow tire occasionally becoming bogged down in the mud. If anyone had seem them, they probably would have thought they were a family.

But they were the furthest thing from family. And when this was all over, she feared she would feel more alone than ever.

Chapter Twelve

A contractor finally got to Marcus's house at the end of the week. He walked around the outside of the building and then he tentatively stepped inside. Marcus followed. The cat ran past them. He needed to keep it out of the house if he could. Or she. The cat was definitely a she. A pregnant she.

"It's going to have to be torn down, Marcus. I'm sorry. I know that isn't what you wanted to hear. The house had issues before the flood. Now it's just hazardous. You need to keep out, and keep everyone else out."

Including that cat.

"You're sure? Even if money is no issue?"

Tad, the contractor, shook his head. "I'll build you anything you want on this land, but this house is done. Not just because of the flood. Main supports are rotted. Some are now broken. The flood took a big chunk out of your foundation. You can't repair this house."

Marcus walked away, glad he'd left Lissa and Oliver with Marissa. He needed time to think, to come to terms with the loss of this dream. He hadn't allowed himself many dreams in life, but this one had been a constant. All the years riding bulls, the money he'd invested in the stock market—it had all been with this one goal in mind. He'd wanted the Brown ranch. Hope Acres, they'd called it.

Truth was, he'd wanted more than the land. He could have bought land anywhere, but he'd wanted this place for one reason and one reason only—the *memories*.

Because of Oliver, that dream had grown into something more. He wanted his son to know a home where people were happy, where they trusted each other and where tempers didn't mean scars. He wanted to be the man who would provide that home, that stability. He'd never thought of this house in terms of children, but with a son, he needed all that this house represented.

He stood by the creek and listened as Tad got in his truck and left. After a few minutes he headed for his own truck. He didn't have a clear plan. When nothing made sense, he drove. This time he didn't head for Bluebonnet or for Alex's place. He wanted to be far away from people who would talk sense into him.

He didn't want to look at Lissa or Oliver and feel conviction.

He wanted a drink. As the thought crashed into his brain, unbidden, he stopped the truck. In the middle of the road he hit the brakes and sat there. No cars were coming. There wasn't anyone for miles around. He sat back, brushing a hand over his face as he contemplated what he'd almost done.

Two days ago he'd met with a lawyer, asking what it would take to get custody of a son when his name wasn't on the birth certificate. Today he was thinking about falling off the wagon. He was the last thing Oliver needed. A house, no matter what it meant to him, wouldn't fix this. A house wouldn't make him the person he wanted to be. For Oliver. He shifted into gear and accelerated on down the road.

At the first intersection he did a U-turn and headed back to town. In the opposite direction of temptation.

When he pulled into the parking lot of the church, he saw Pastor Matthews with a few other men surveying the roof of the church. It needed to be replaced. It could have waited another six months or so, but the rain had brought about some weak spots and exposed leaks.

Marcus got out and joined the group that had gathered. They stood on the front lawn, looking up at the steeple.

"Marcus, glad you showed up. We're trying to decide if the steeple can handle another ten years or if we should repair it, as well as the roof." Pastor Matthews winked, giving Marcus a clear clue as to how he felt about the steeple. He had wanted it repaired for a year or more, but the men of the church had stubbornly dug in their heels and said to wait.

Marcus ignored the meaningful look the pastor gave him. "It's leaning a bit. I know you all will do the right thing. And I'll do what I can to help."

"Now that you're a family man, it appears we'll have you paying more attention to these things." Dan Wilson, Marissa's grandfather, laughed as he made the comment.

Marcus didn't respond. He didn't have words.

Pastor Matthews shook a few hands and excused himself from the meeting. "Marcus and I need to talk about some other problems around town. Maybe we can think of a way to help the folks that were hardest hit."

The other men wandered off and Marcus followed his pastor around the side of the building. There hadn't been much wind during the storm, but enough to take off some shingles.

"What's going on?" Duncan Matthews asked as he stopped to survey one of the older windows that hadn't been replaced in the remodeling they'd done over the past few years.

"I can't do this."

"Can't help the community?" the pastor asked.

"I can't do this to Oliver. I don't want to hurt him."

Serious brown eyes studied him, waiting for him to spill it.

"I'm one step away from falling off the wagon. I don't have a home." That was Marcus's truth. It was his reality.

"Oh, I see. Did you fall off the wagon?"

"Not yet."

"But you're determined to try?" He said it without a smile.

"No, I'm not determined. But it could happen. And what would that do to him?" Marcus slid a hand through his hair. "I don't want to take Oliver from Lissa. She's raised him. He has a bond with her."

"I can understand that you're worried. Would it make you feel better if I said I wasn't? You aren't the same man you were a few years ago."

Marcus clenched his jaw. "I know I'm not.

But how do I take that boy from the woman who has been a mother to him?"

"How about the two of you talk and work something out? Maybe share custody…"

"She lives in San Antonio and I live in Blue-bonnet." And he couldn't imagine her being gone. That was a complication he hadn't planned on. He'd never planned on a woman changing all of his plans, all of his goals.

Pastor Matthews grinned. "I guess you could marry her."

Floored would not have been a strong enough word for what Marcus felt when Duncan made that suggestion. Marriage had to be the furthest thing from his mind. And the worst possible option.

"*Marry* her?"

Duncan shrugged. "Seems perfect to me. Two people who both love a child and who seem to have some type of feelings for each other."

"I don't love her." Marcus stuttered the words.

Again the pastor lifted a casual shoulder. "Of course not."

Of course he didn't love her. "She's a thorn in my side who happened to turn my world upside down."

"Tell me how you really feel, cowboy."

The words, softly spoken in that all too familiar voice. He cringed and turned.

Lissa stood at the corner of the building. Fortunately alone. He shoved his hat back and pulled it forward, trying to find the best way out of this mess. She didn't wait; she headed his way and the coward of a pastor hightailed it out of there.

Lissa, with those bright blue eyes and a smile that said *Gotcha*, stopped in front of him. "Oh, don't get all red in the face. Of course you don't want to marry me. Thorn in the side, though? That seems a little unfair."

He sighed. "Yeah, that was unfair. Maybe I was being too lenient."

"I'm the disaster of a woman who crashed into your life and made you face mistakes, and the future. And being the cowboy you are, you'd rather have gone on your merry way as a bachelor with no worries."

"I guess that about nails it. Where's Oliver?"

"At least you're honest about your feelings for me," she said, letting him off the hook. "Oliver is around front with Lucy. Why? Do you have more you need to say to me?"

"No, or maybe I do need to say more. You're not a thorn. Or a disaster. If I was a man who could marry…"

"If you weren't punishing yourself for being Jesse Palermo's offspring."

"Yes." He had to give her points for being blunt. "If I wasn't Jesse Palermo's son. If I wasn't an alcoholic. If I wasn't a sorry excuse for a human being, and if I could ever be good enough for someone like you… I would marry you."

"That was sweet. Not exactly a proposal, but sweet. And because I don't want a roller-coaster ride of a relationship, I'm very glad you're not asking."

They stood there facing each other, and he couldn't help feeling empty as they said those words to one another. Lissa bit down on her bottom lip and looked away, and he wondered if she felt it, too. As if the two of them, because of their pasts, would always be missing out on what other people took for granted.

Or maybe he was just extra negative today because of the house, Oliver and feeling the worst case of temptation he'd felt since he quit drinking. And it wasn't alcohol tempting him. It was her. His heart did a strange stutter at the realization.

"Lissa, I…"

"I know you hired a lawyer to take Oliver. I get it. He's your son and you have the right.

I'm begging you to not take him completely." Her eyes welled up with tears.

He reached out and brushed them away, and then his finger slid down her cheek to her chin. He tipped her face, wishing he could kiss her. Wishing he could do more than be the man who hurt her.

"I'm not taking Oliver. I met with the lawyer to see about custody. He needs to be with you. I've set up a trust fund and child support. We can work on visits."

"Marcus, he needs you."

"Yeah, I guess he probably does. A dad is important. Or so I've been told. We'll make sure he spends time here. But he needs more than I can give him. I'm a recovering alcoholic who doesn't have a home."

"Right. Of course." She stood on tiptoe and kissed his cheek.

Marcus tilted his head, capturing her mouth in a last, sweet kiss.

"I have a new joke." Oliver rounded the corner of the church and skidded to a halt.

Lissa pulled back from Marcus and what had felt like a goodbye kiss. She hated goodbyes. Most especially this one. She blinked, because she wasn't going to cry. She wasn't going to let him get to her.

But it might have been too late for that. Because he had become the unexpected. Not only was he not the person she'd thought he would be, but the way he touched her so profoundly had taken her by surprise.

In two weeks he'd become a person she trusted. And against all odds, she'd let him into her heart. No. He'd taken her heart captive.

"Were you two kissing?" Oliver said it as if it had to be the most disgusting thing ever. "Gross."

Marcus laughed. "Don't worry, Oliver, I'll wash my cheek real good and I probably won't get cooties."

"The girl is the one who gets cooties," Lissa countered, because it felt safer to have this conversation than to think about the future.

The joking and the friendship proved they could co-parent Oliver. They would work out visits. They would probably see each other often. On the inside she cringed, because seeing him often might be the hardest part of this entire plan.

"What's your joke?" Marcus asked, picking up his son and tweaking his nose.

Oliver's smile split his face, exposing the dimple that made him look so much like his father. "Knock knock."

"Who's there?" Marcus almost grinned as he asked.

Lissa watched the two of them. Marcus trying hard to be serious and Oliver making a funny face, probably hoping that would tip the scale in his favor.

"Banana."

"Banana who?"

"Banana…" Oliver grimaced. He bit down on his lip. "I think I forgot."

Marcus laughed, and Oliver did, too. "Kid, I think that's the best one yet. I think we should get Alex and go ride a pony."

"I made you laugh?" Oliver grabbed his hand.

"Yeah, you made me laugh." Marcus set Oliver back on his feet and took him by the hand. "Knock knock."

"Who's there?" Oliver moved in close to his side.

"Pony."

Oliver grinned big. "Pony who?"

"Pony who wants you to ride him."

Oliver fell over laughing. A belly laugh that was contagious. "That's not even a joke."

Marcus took off his hat and put it on his son's head. "Nope, but it made you laugh. And it was definitely better than 'banana, I can't think of the rest.'"

Lissa followed the two of them, picturing them as Oliver got older. And Marcus… He would get older, too. They would probably rodeo together. Marcus would teach his son to ride and to be a rancher. And someday Oliver would choose this life over the life she offered in the city.

It unsettled her, all of these changes. For as long as she could remember, she'd maintained an orderly life. She set goals. She worked hard to keep everything and everyone in a neat box. Friends. Family. Career.

Oliver. She'd kept him in a box, too. He was Sammy's son. But deep down, he'd become her child. She loved him the way any mom would love a child. She needed to tell him that.

Marcus was offering a way for her to continue that relationship, but it meant taking Oliver from Bluebonnet and from the family here. Everything had become infinitely more complicated.

"I'm heading back to Alex's," Marcus told her as they neared the front of the church. "How did the two of you get here?"

"Marissa. She's inside giving a hand with the evening meal. I wanted to see Doc. He asked if I could help him for a few days. And since I only have a few more days in Bluebonnet, I thought I'd make myself useful."

"Do you mind if Oliver and I head back to the ranch, then? I thought we'd have a riding lesson."

"You don't have to ask permission to take your son with you, Marcus."

"No, of course not." He placed a hand on Marcus's shoulder. "But I'm also not going to take off and not discuss plans with you."

They were co-parenting. Okay, she could handle that. Step one in the two of them raising Oliver together. And *not* together. With a pang, she watched Marcus and Oliver leave, and then she headed inside to find Doc.

She met up with Marissa in the hall.

"Lissa, you okay?" Marissa asked as she approached. "Did Marcus do something?"

She smiled at that. Yes, he'd done several somethings. And it had ended with a kiss so sweet it had felt as if her heart would never recover.

"Of course—" she hesitated "—not."

Marissa slipped an arm around Lissa's waist and the two walked together. "What did he do?"

"He talked to a lawyer about custody of Oliver. I know that makes sense. I just hadn't thought about it."

"He isn't all bad, you know."

"I know he isn't. But no matter what, this is going to hurt."

"I hope that it doesn't have to hurt. And I know Marcus well enough to know he'll try to do the best thing for all three of you. He's been building himself up as the bad twin for a long time. He's the rebel. He's the one who struggled in school. He fought anyone who dared to challenge him. He rode some of the meanest bulls in the country. All to prove that he is cold, angry, bad to the bone. But he isn't."

"No, he isn't. And that's made this whole process so much harder than I thought it would be. I thought I'd come here, Marcus would be the person I'd pictured."

"Angry, dysfunctional and a drunk?" Marissa asked.

"Yes, I guess. And instead…"

"He's angry, charming, sweet."

"Stop." Lissa held up a hand. "I just want him to be a dad to Oliver."

"Of course. So you'll be leaving at the end of the week?" Marissa stopped outside Doc's office. "I think Doc was hoping you'd change your mind and stay here."

"I can't stay." She said it with less conviction than in weeks past, because leaving now meant leaving something more than a job. She was abandoning a community and people she'd come to care about in the past two weeks. She would be leaving behind the friendships. And Marcus.

"We all wish you would," Marissa said. "Some of us more than others, I think. And that's something I never thought I'd believe about Marcus. I really thought he'd be an old man living on that farm, no wife, no kids, just his grouchy old self."

"I think that's still his plan. Except he'll have Oliver."

"Right, of course. He'll have Oliver."

Lissa reached to open the door to the clinic. "I'm going to help Doc."

"For what it's worth, I'm sorry. And I think you're the best thing to ever happen to my brother-in-law."

It didn't matter what either of them said. Marcus had made it pretty clear how he felt about her. She was the thorn in his side. And she understood how he might feel that way. She'd upended his world. She and Oliver had stayed and he'd been forced to take on the role of father.

And…he'd kissed her. She couldn't stop thinking about that kiss. He might have said no to her in his life, but that kiss said yes.

Chapter Thirteen

It was toward the end of the week and Marcus didn't like to think about time slipping away. Oliver and Lissa would be leaving in a matter of days. And he would miss them. He didn't want to admit that to himself, to his twin, to anyone.

"I'm going to donate my paintings." He said it as he drove toward town, Alex in the passenger seat. Oliver rode in the back, but he wasn't paying attention.

"The guy who never let anyone know he painted is going to donate them now? For...?" Alex fiddled with the window.

Marcus locked the windows because Alex had to be about ten years old when it came to pushing buttons. Literally and figuratively.

"I'm going to put them in the church auction for the flood fund."

"I would say that's a big step toward adulthood."

"Thanks, bro," he said. "That means a lot coming from you."

Alex glanced in the back seat before he spoke. "You're also an idiot."

Marcus shot him a surprised look.

Alex didn't laugh. He didn't crack a smile. "I mean it. You're messing up."

"I'm not having this conversation with you," Marcus ground out.

"Well, too bad. Because you're going to have it with me."

"Are you two fighting?" Oliver asked from the back.

"Yes."

"No." Both brothers answered. And then they glared at each other again.

"Is Maria getting married?" Oliver asked. "I told her I'd be her ring bearer."

"Married?" This time they answered in unison.

Marcus glanced back and then returned his attention to the road. "Why do you think that?"

"Because Jake came back yesterday. He was at Aunt Essie's talking to Maria." Oliver stopped talking.

"What?" the two brothers asked.

"I'm not supposed to tell."

Marcus stared into the rearview mirror. "So

you're *not* going to tell us how you know they're getting married?"

Oliver shook his head.

Alex laughed a little. "Maria said that guy only planned to stay a few days, but then all of a sudden she wanted to introduce him to the family. It sure looks like he's settled in. Lucy said he's staying with them through the summer."

"He's too old for her," Marcus insisted.

"He's six years older than she is. That isn't too old. She's almost twenty."

They let the conversation go. Oliver wasn't talking.

Marcus drove them through Bluebonnet Springs and to the work area where men from the church planned to meet up for the day. Spring Street in Bluebonnet Springs, aptly named because it ran parallel to the spring, had suffered the most damage in the flood. Several homes had significant flood damage.

"Now, you're going to be good and stay with me. Right, Oliver?" Marcus asked as he got his son out of the booster seat. "Lissa gave us all the rules for being safe. Gloves. No stepping on boards that might have nails."

Oliver nodded and the two of them hurried to catch up to Alex. They had to step around debris as they made their way. Amazing that one little creek could do so much damage.

There were several men congregated at the front of a house that had been built a hundred years ago and had probably been through its share of floods. The siding of the house had never been updated, so it was still wood. The paint, in part due to age and in part due to the flooding, had been chipped away, leaving big sections of bare wood slats. Marcus walked up to the group of men who were surveying the property. Pastor Matthews, Alex, Lucy's husband, Dane Scott, and others. Jake, the boyfriend of Maria, was there, too. Marcus made sure to give him a glare that would remind him she had two brothers who ought to be asked before he went proposing marriage.

Oliver slid in next to him, his hand in Marcus's.

"What are we looking at?" he asked.

"A mess," Pastor Matthews responded. "But not one we can't handle. The floodwaters soaked the old plaster walls in the Moore house. The linoleum on the kitchen floor peeled up and the carpet in the bedrooms will have to be taken up. The biggest problem is the mold and the plaster walls. That about sums up every house on this block."

"My dad is going to auction off his paintings to help." Oliver yanked on Marcus's hand as he made the announcement. Obviously he had been listening to their conversation in the truck. "Aren't you, Dad? You paint all kinds of pictures."

Marcus choked a little. Oliver stared up at him, eyes all innocent and sweet. Marcus didn't know what emotion to process first. His son had just called him *dad* for the first time. *Dad.* The word meant a lot. It meant responsibility, never giving up on a kid, being there for him.

And he'd just had his paintings outed to a group of men he wouldn't have considered telling.

Dane gave him a curious look. Alex just laughed. Pastor Matthews appeared to be trying to hide a smile.

But all that mattered right now was that Oliver had called him dad. He wanted to shout it to the world. He wanted to call Lissa. That thought stopped him in his tracks. She'd become a habit. Maybe more of a temptation than his old habits. She was the first thing he thought of when something happened, good or bad.

"Maybe we should get some work done." Marcus glanced around the lawn of the house. Trash from the flood littered the yards and even the sidewalks. "I have big trash bags and extra pairs of gloves if anyone wants to help me start getting some of this cleaned up. I've got the trailer hooked to my truck so I can go from here to the Dumpsters set up at the school."

Oliver yanked on his hand again. "But, Dad, tell them about your art. Especially that bull painting. It looks like crayons, but it isn't. Tell them about that one."

"We probably need to get some work done, son," he said. But he managed to smile because Oliver had about the happiest look on his face. "You have to be careful. There could be nails and sharp metal. Don't pick up anything unless you ask."

"I could pick up sticks," Oliver offered.

"Okay, you can pick up sticks. We'll make one pile for those." Marcus handed Oliver a pair of gloves. "I found these at the feed store. They're your size."

The gloves looked just like the ones Marcus wore. They looked like father and son, and now that Oliver had called him dad, it truly *felt* like it, as well.

They walked down the block, picking up trash as they went. There were boards, tree limbs, even parts of buildings scattered where the flood had deposited debris it brought downstream.

Alex joined them, bringing extra of the

large, heavy-duty trash bags. "I thought you might like company."

"I'm pretty happy with the company I have." Marcus nodded in Oliver's direction. He stopped to look around. "Some of this we could pile up and burn."

"That's probably a good idea."

All of a sudden, Marcus paused. "Hey, Alex, do you hear that?"

"What am I listening for?"

Marcus put a finger up. "Listen."

Oliver ran to his side, dropping small branches as he went.

"I hear it, too. I hear it whining." The little boy, his arms holding the few sticks that hadn't been dropped, stopped and tilted his head to listen.

"I think it might be in the ditch," Alex offered.

The boy dropped the remaining sticks and raced for the ditch as fast as his little legs could pump.

Marcus hurried to catch up with him. "Oliver, be careful. We don't know what all is down there."

Water still stood, even after nearly a week. Marcus stepped carefully and pulled away some of the branches and trash that had built up near a culvert.

"A puppy?" Oliver asked. "Can I see?"

Marcus squatted to look in the culvert. Dark and filled with debris, it didn't look like anything that an animal could live in. His son got close to his side.

Alex leaned in behind them with the flashlight from his phone. "Let me help."

Bright eyes glowed from the narrow confines of the culvert. Marcus reached in, letting the puppy sniff his hand before he managed to get hold of the animal, hauling him out by the scruff of his neck. The puppy yelped and cried, but they got him out in the light, where they had a better look at him.

"Puppy, you are in poor shape," Marcus whispered to the tiny animal. "And no bigger than a minute."

"Looks like a Labrador, although it's hard to tell with all of that mud. And he's all skin and bones." Alex ran a hand down the puppy's back. "I think you should take him to Doc Parker."

"I'm sure Doc would appreciate a four-legged patient."

"Better manners than some of his two-legged patients." Alex stood back up, grinning down at him.

Marcus stared for a moment, as if he was looking at himself in the mirror. Except for one big difference. Alex had found something that had changed his life. He'd found Marissa. He was happy, with himself, his life, his faith.

"You okay?" Alex asked.

Marcus stood, cradling the puppy against him. "Yeah, I'm fine."

He looked around, missing Oliver, who had been glued to his side. "Oliver?"

The little boy was on his hands and knees, crawling into the round drainpipe. Marcus shoved the puppy at Alex.

"Hey, get out of there!" He reached for him, but it was too late. Oliver screamed and jumped back.

His son raised a hand, gashed across his palm. Blood and debris mixed and ran down his arm. Marcus prayed it looked worse than it was. He picked up the boy and took the handkerchief Alex had ready for him.

"Hang on, buddy, let me take a look." Marcus dabbed at the cut with the handkerchief and sucked in a breath at what he saw. The cut was deep and bleeding profusely.

"I want Lissa," Oliver cried against his shoulder. "I want Lissa."

"We'll get Lissa." Marcus trudged up the hill and headed for his truck. "Alex, can you call Lissa and Doc Parker? Tell them I'm heading to Doc's clinic."

"Want me to ride with you?"

Marcus shook his head. "We're good. Can you unhook the trailer off my truck? I'll get Marcus into the seat. There's a towel in the back seat that will work better than this handkerchief."

Marcus gently settled Oliver in the seat and buckled the seat belt. The little boy was sobbing, tears dripping down a face that was dirty from working in the yard.

"I unhooked the trailer. Do you need anything else?" Alex appeared at Marcus's side. The other men were behind him. "I don't mind going with you."

"I'll head over, but I'll call you after Doc has a look."

It took less than five minutes to get to Doc's clinic.

"Here we are," he told Oliver. The little boy didn't look good. His face was pale and the tears had dried up. "Hey, you're okay, little man. I promise, you're fine."

"I don't like blood." Oliver shuddered.

"I don't blame you, but in a few minutes Doc will have you all cleaned up. I'm sorry, Oliver. I shouldn't have had you down there."

"I thought there might be another puppy. Like a brother."

He unbuckled his son and pulled him into

his arms. As they headed for the door of the clinic, Lissa hurried out to meet them.

"Lissa is here," Marcus said as he reached for the door, trying to be careful not to jostle Oliver. He didn't know what to do when the little boy started to cry again. "Did I hurt you?"

Oliver shook his head. "I just want Lissa."

Of course. Marcus understood that. He wasn't much of a comforter. Lissa was. He could vouch for that. She took Oliver from him and held him close.

"What in the world did you do, wrestle with glass?" She whispered close to his ear as she cuddled him against her.

"I had to save the puppy and see if it had a brother," he explained. He glanced over her shoulder and looked at Marcus. "Where's the puppy?"

"The puppy is in the truck. I'll get him in a minute. We want Lissa and Doc to check you out first."

Oliver sniffled and wiped his face with his good hand. "Maybe Doc could help him, too?"

As if on cue, Doc Parker appeared in the doorway. "What's all this ruckus? Oliver, are you having a bad day?"

Oliver nodded. "And we found a hurt puppy. Marcus needs to get him so you can fix him."

Doc laughed at that. "I'm not much of a veterinarian, but I can take a look after we've taken care of you. Let's get you to an exam room."

Marcus stepped back. Lissa handed Oliver over to Doc and remained in the waiting room, her blue eyes bright, focused on him.

"I'll get the puppy." He couldn't help that his voice was gruff with emotion. He'd never felt this helpless in his life. He'd never needed to be away from a place as much as he wanted out of that clinic.

"Marcus."

"He called me dad. I didn't know it would feel like this, to go from Marcus to dad." It had all become real in the last hour or so. The word *dad* had changed things in a way that Oliver showing up in his life hadn't.

"Don't you leave," Lissa said with meaning, as if she knew what he was thinking.

"I'm not leaving. I won't leave."

She disappeared through the door and he sat down, needing a minute to get his head on straight. On his watch, Oliver had gotten hurt. Marcus knew that kids got hurt. But he couldn't shake the image of Oliver, pale and hurting and wanting Lissa. Not him. *Lissa.*

Lissa found Marcus sitting on the tailgate of his truck holding something in a horse blanket. She sat down next to him and reached for the puppy. The animal squirmed in her lap but then turned to lick her hand.

"Is he okay?" Marcus asked as they sat there.

"Yes, he is. He needed ten stitches. It was deep and it needed to be cleaned out. Doc gave us antibiotics, just because of the floodwater and not knowing what all could have been in that muck he reached through.

"What about you? Are you okay?" she asked.

He gave her a sideways look. "I'm fine."

Right. Of course he was. Lissa didn't push. She knew he'd been shaken, but she suspected there was more to it than the gash on Oliver's hand.

"I'm glad you're okay, because he's asking for you. I don't want you going in there looking like you just poured a bowl of cereal and discovered there's no milk."

"I'm sure that isn't the look on my face." He rubbed his hands down his face, as if that would relieve the tension from his expression.

"Oh, it is the look. I promise it is. Doc said you can bring the puppy in and he'll take care of him."

"I think he's hungry more than anything. He's skin and bones."

She lifted the puppy and gave it a good look,

and then she smiled. "It is a cute thing. Good thing you have plenty of room for animals. Oliver has already decided he wants to keep it. I told him you'd have to at least try to find the owners and, also, he'll have to make sure it's okay with you."

"With me? If Oliver is keeping the puppy, it's going home with him."

"We can't have pets. The puppy stays with you and the cat."

He hopped off the tailgate and walked away from her. She let him go. When he turned, she saw all of the confusion, worry and pain written into his expression.

"When are you leaving?" he asked.

"Two days. But we'll be back. Remember, you want weekends and to share holidays, summer breaks. It's like an amicable divorce."

"Is there any such thing?"

Lissa shrugged. She had never thought about it before. Now that she did, she realized everyone got hurt. There was no party who walked away completely unscathed.

Marcus narrowed the distance he'd put between them. "When he got hurt, it wasn't me he wanted. It was you. You're the one who makes him feel safe. You make him feel secure. I'm just fun for the time being because I have an old dog and ponies. Dogs and ponies aren't going to sustain him forever. When he gets sick or hurt or even lonely, he's going to want you."

"I think you're trying to find a problem when there isn't one." She gave him a long, level look. "He's a typical little boy. He asked for the person who has been a mom to him. If you're worried about how you handled this, you did what any dad would do. You didn't panic and you got him to the doctor."

"Oh, I panicked," he admitted drily.

"He didn't know it."

"No, I guess he didn't." He stepped a little closer and she could see the anguish in his eyes.

"You are his dad. And he does need you."

"But he needs you more. He needs a mom." He nodded in the direction of the clinic. "We should go in. I don't want him to be alone, wondering where we are. He worries, you know."

"I know." She had stayed awake with him the nights he'd cried himself to sleep and the nights he'd awoken with bad dreams.

They walked back through the clinic, Marcus carrying the puppy, who whined pitifully from inside the blanket. From room two she could hear Oliver telling Doc Parker all about the way they'd heard that puppy crying and then rescued him from the pipe under the road. When they entered the room with the puppy, Oliver's eyes lit up. He was sitting on the bed, his injured hand bandaged and cradled in his other arm. She knew it hurt. But the puppy seemed to take his mind off the pain.

"Can you fix him, Doc?" Oliver asked as Doc Parker peeked inside the horse blanket.

"That's a fine-looking pup, Oliver. Looks like he might be a Labrador. Chocolate-colored, I'd say. But first we need to wash the mud off him and see how he looks."

"He was holding up one leg," Oliver offered. "But we got him out of that hole in the ground."

Doc took the puppy. "I'm taking him to my utility room to clean him up, and then we'll give him a real examination. But I think he's going to be just fine, Oliver. I think, more than anything, this guy needs something to eat."

"Me, too," Oliver said.

Doc left and Oliver lost his mojo. He curled up, holding his arm.

"Knock knock," Marcus said as he pulled up a stool and sat down next to the bed.

Oliver grinned. "Who's there?"

"Interrupting cow."

"Interrupting cow—"

"Moo," Marcus said before the boy could get out the word *who*.

"Hey!" Oliver said. "You didn't let me ask. Interrupting cow—"

"Moo," Marcus said again.

"What are you doing that for?" Oliver was still laughing.

"I'm an interrupting cow," Marcus told him.

They both laughed, and then Oliver leaned forward and threw his good arm around Marcus. "You're a funny dad."

Lissa's heart melted and she brushed away the tears that trickled down her cheeks. This was why she had come. She'd come here to give Oliver this gift. The gift of a father. If only Marcus could see that he was a dad. He was exactly the man Oliver needed. He might be a little broken, a little banged up emotionally, but deep down, he was good.

It felt as if her heart was colliding with her common sense as she watched him with his son. She'd come here knowing what she wanted for her life, and now what she wanted looked a lot like the man sitting with Oliver telling knock-knock jokes.

Doc returned with the puppy. He had a towel wrapped around the little dog, and sure enough, it did look like a chocolate-colored Labrador. He handed the animal over to Oliver, cautioning the little boy to hold tight but to watch his own injured paw.

"Is his leg hurt?"

"I think just a sore paw. Nothing appears to be broken. Now, I'm not a vet, so I would watch him over the next couple of days. Give him water and small amounts of food."

"I'm going to name him Buddy." Oliver leaned down and the puppy licked his cheek.

"I think that's a real good name. Now, don't forget to keep your hand clean and dry. Lissa will watch for infection." Doc looked from Lissa to Marcus. "Anything else?"

"I think we're set." Marcus picked up the puppy and handed it to Lissa. "You might want to make sure you can have pets."

"Marcus." Her warning came too late. He simply hadn't thought. She'd already told him she couldn't have pets.

"But Buddy can't live in an apartment." Oliver scooted to the edge of the bed. His dark eyes were bright with tears. "He's a country dog and he wants to stay here. He likes to run in fields and play fetch."

"Oliver." Marcus shook his head. "I don't know what to say."

"You're my dad." Oliver sobbed into Marcus's side. "I want to ride horses and learn to rope."

"You'll get to do those things," Marcus promised. "And I'll learn when to keep my mouth shut."

Doc Parker stood at the door watching them. "On-the-job training is how parents learn. You can buy books, attend seminars, but none of it is going to make sense without real-life experience."

Marcus picked up Oliver, holding him as Lissa stood back, the puppy wiggling in her arms.

The whole situation seemed more complicated than ever. Because they were all in over their heads and feeling things they hadn't expected to feel.

Chapter Fourteen

Marcus pulled up to the community church as the bell pealed across the countryside. He loved the sound of church bells. The good old country kind that a person could hear a mile away on a clear summer morning. As he got out of his truck, he spotted Essie. Lissa and Oliver had just arrived, as well.

Oliver saw him, said something to Lissa and then ran for Marcus. Little arms went around Marcus's waist, holding tight. Who would have thought in the matter of a few weeks that his son's hugs would change everything for him?

"Can I see Buddy today?" Oliver asked when Marcus picked his son up.

"I think that's an option, little man. Alex and Marissa invited us for lunch, and Buddy is there waiting to see you. How's your hand?"

Oliver held out his hand, palm up. Marcus

had to give Doc credit, his seams could rival the ones sewn by the quilting circle.

"Lissa said you had to doze down your house. Does that mean knock it down to the ground?" Oliver looked at him, eyes narrowed.

"I'm afraid so."

"Will you build a new one for us to live in?" Oliver asked, the question coming out of left field.

Marcus stopped walking toward the church to stare down into dark eyes that matched his. "I haven't really decided. I loved that old farmhouse. It meant a lot to me."

"If you build a new house, can Lissa live there, too?" Oliver asked. "Is it going to be a big house? With a dog door for Buddy and Lucky? And I'll have a bedroom they can sleep in. And Lissa can have her own room."

Marcus lowered Oliver so the two of them could walk side by side. He had to admit, he liked it when his son tried to match small steps to Marcus's larger steps.

"I'm sure it can have a dog door." He avoided answering the question about Lissa. He also wouldn't say yes to the dogs sleeping with Oliver, although he figured it would probably happen.

"I bet I could crawl through a dog door," Oliver continued, totally oblivious to the fact that Marcus was lost in thought. "Knock knock."

Marcus jerked his thoughts back to the present and his son. "Who's there?"

"Dog."

"Dog who?"

Oliver stopped walking. "Dog who got stuck in the doggy door."

"I think you're totally missing the point of knock-knock jokes," Marcus told him. "Hurry up, we'll be late for church."

Lissa and Essie had gone on ahead of them and were now waiting on the church steps. Lissa looked… He paused because he had to decide how she looked. Like a painting, that was how he had to describe her as she stood on the steps of the church, the breeze lifting her hair around her face, her expression soft as she watched Oliver. The face of a mother.

The face of a woman that in any other lifetime he would have fallen in love with. He guessed a man couldn't have everything. He could dream. If it was that easy, he'd dream himself up as a man who could be the person she wanted in her life.

"Lissa, we're going to Alex's for lunch today." Oliver reached for her hand as they hurried up the stairs.

Marcus watched as she bent to talk to Oliver,

straightening his collar and brushing a hand through his hair. When she looked up, her eyes were misty with unshed tears. He couldn't be the man she was looking for, but he could do one thing for her. He could make sure she felt secure with Oliver.

They sat with Marcus's family. It wasn't easy to focus on the sermon. Not with Oliver and Lissa next to him, knowing that he had to take care of things. Today. If they continued on the way they were, it would only get more difficult. He wouldn't want to let go. Funny that the sermon should be about letting go. Letting go of our dreams in exchange for God's plans. Letting go of insecurities for the peace that God gives. Letting go of fear, because we are more than conquerors through Christ who strengthens us.

But the sermon was also about allowing God to be in control. That was the part he had a hard time with. His entire childhood had been controlled by a man with a quick temper and a hard fist. He was old enough and had come far enough in his faith to understand that God gave free will. It was still difficult to let God take control of his life.

He didn't feel good about the fact that he'd never been so glad to have a sermon end. When he got up to head out, Essie followed.

"Ants in your pants?" she asked.

"Aunt in my business?" he whispered back.

She laughed. "That's a good one. And you bet I'm in your business. I didn't pay enough attention when you were young, so I have a lot of lost time to make up for."

"I'm fine. And you paid plenty of attention. When he allowed it."

"The sermon was about control. That bothers you, doesn't it?"

"Not at all." He stopped to look around for Oliver. His son was talking to Lucy and Dane's daughter Issy.

"That boy is something else. If you mess this up, Marcus, I'm not sure what I'll do with you."

"I'm not going to mess this up. I'm going to do the right thing for my son. He belongs with Lissa. He deserves the kind of life she can give him. And they deserve a secure, happy life."

"You're doing the easy thing for yourself," Essie snapped. "I have to go. I suddenly have a bad headache."

She hurried away and he would have guessed her head was just fine. He turned and Lissa was behind him. From her narrow-eyed expression, she'd overheard the conversation with his aunt.

"What is that all about?" she asked.

"No beating around the bush?" Marcus sighed. "I think you and my aunt are cut from the same cloth."

Her mouth quirked at the corner. "Thank you for the compliment."

"You're welcome."

"Should we talk now or later?" she asked.

"I think later." He searched the church and spotted Oliver at the doors with Issy. The two were talking, becoming cousins.

He hadn't thought about it, about the family Oliver had gained when he became part of the Palermos. They'd always been dysfunctional. Growing up, Marcus had been a pariah of sorts. He had gotten used to the fact that girls wanted to date him because they'd considered him a bad boy. Parents hadn't wanted their daughters to be seen with him.

He searched for his sisters and saw them talking with people from church. Alex and Marissa had taught children's church today. When had this happened? When had they all become so functional and respected? They were a family. A good family.

"Are you okay?" Lissa asked.

"I'm good, just had a moment." Nothing had changed in that moment. It had just been a realization of sorts. "I think it would be easier if you go sooner rather than later."

"You want us to leave?"

"Isn't that your plan? To leave today?"

She looked confused. "Yes, of course. We can leave right after lunch. But I'm not telling Oliver. That's on you."

"Don't worry, I'll tell him. And it's June. We can spend more time together this summer. Before school starts in August."

"Of course you can."

He had avoided relationships for most of his life, but he knew an angry woman when he saw one. He decided escape was his best bet. "I'll meet you at the ranch."

He watched as she went to gather up Oliver. She bent to tell him they were leaving. He heard her tell him they would see Issy at Alex and Marissa's. Marcus joined them, thinking he might be able to make it easier.

"We have to leave now?" Oliver complained as they crossed the lawn to the parking lot. He was glancing back, looking for all of his new friends.

"You want to see Buddy, don't you?" Marcus asked.

Oliver nodded, but he didn't look too thrilled, or convinced. "Issy said she'd show me her pony again."

Marcus helped Oliver into the rental car. "I bet she will. How's that hand?"

Oliver looked at his hand. "It's still good. I bumped it and thought it would bleed again. But it didn't. Does that mean I can ride a horse?"

"I'm not sure. It might. I'll meet you at Alex's." He closed the door and Lissa was still standing there, her expression thoughtful. "What?"

She shrugged. "I think you want us to leave because you don't want to say goodbye. You love him."

"He's my son."

Her gaze softened. "Oh, Marcus, you're such an idiot."

"Yeah, I guess I am." He kissed her cheek. "Meet you at the ranch."

He walked away, wishing he didn't have to. He wished he could be the hero who saved the day. Just once. He didn't want to be the man who always felt as if he'd failed the people in his life. He wanted to be the dad a son could count on. Lissa made him want to be the man a woman could count on.

The ride to the ranch took fifteen minutes. It felt more like an hour. As he pulled up to the ranch, he saw Lissa getting out of the car, then glancing into the back seat. The wind lifted her hair and swirled her floral skirt around her legs.

He headed her way to see if she needed help.

She was the one thing he knew he wouldn't get past. He'd dealt with his childhood, the loss of his voice, his parents. But her... He shook his head as he got out of his truck. He wouldn't get over her.

Marcus walked up behind her and peered over her shoulder.

"He needs a nap. He hasn't been sleeping well," Lissa said, indicating the sleeping child in the back seat.

Marcus nodded, understanding. He hadn't been sleeping so well himself. "I'll carry him inside."

He scooped his son up from the booster in the back seat of the car. Lissa hurried ahead of him to open the front door so that he could carry Oliver inside. Maria had gotten to the house early and she brought a blanket to cover her nephew.

"Where's Jake?" Marcus asked quietly.

"On his way back from visiting his parents. Marcus, give him a chance. He wants to talk to you all."

"I am giving him a chance. I just don't want you to be hurt."

She kissed his cheek. "I won't be hurt. I love him and he loves me. This is the right plan for my life. I know where I'm going and what God wants. And Jake is part of the plan. We aren't rushing into anything, but we know what we want."

"Good." He gave her a quick hug. "But tell him he owes us a conversation, Alex and me."

"Of course he does." She glanced down at her sleeping nephew and her lips pulled up. "He's not just an eavesdropper. He is a blabbermouth."

"He is." He felt a tug on his heart.

Maria looked up, studying Marcus's face. "Don't mess this up."

"My family has a lot of faith in me."

"I have faith in you. You don't have faith in yourself. And sometimes I wonder if you've ever given anything to God," she said with far more wisdom than he expected from his little sister.

"I try, Maria. I do try."

He left his little sister to care for his son, and he went in search of Lissa. He found her on the front porch. She smiled when he walked out the door, and she patted the seat next to her. He couldn't sit next to her. If he did, he'd never want to let her go.

Marcus realized the flaw in his plan. He wanted to make things right for her, but he also didn't want to lose either of them. They were going back to their lives in San Antonio. He would resume his life here in Bluebonnet Springs. He and Lissa would see each other on occasion, and Oliver would spend time here. But it wouldn't be the same.

Never in a million years would he have imagined this goodbye being one of the hardest in his life. It had been easy three weeks ago. Now he wasn't sure what it felt like to have a broken heart. He doubted he had ever experienced one. But what he felt at that moment, telling her goodbye…it was pretty close.

Lissa had known coming to Bluebonnet Springs that this would never end well. In the past few weeks she'd suspected it would end worse than she'd expected because she hadn't expected to feel anything other than resentment for Marcus Palermo. That had changed as she'd gotten to know him. She took a breath at the inadequacy of that word. She'd fallen in love with him.

She watched as he paced the porch and then faced her, an anguished look on his face. She wondered if she wore the same expression because she knew that was what she felt.

"You might as well tell me what it is you want to say. If you've changed your mind and you want him here with you, I understand. He is your son. Just tell me because I want time to lick my wounds before I have to leave." She couldn't look at him. She couldn't accept the hand he offered.

"Don't be ridiculous, I'm not taking him from you."

At those carefully spoken words in his gruff whisper of a voice, she looked up. "Okay, then what is it?"

"I talked to a lawyer about giving you legal custody. But I want more than that for him. I want you to be his mom."

Her heart stopped. "You what?"

Red flooded his cheeks. "No. Not like that. I want you to adopt him. I want him to know that no one can take him from you."

"You want me to adopt him?" She shook her head, not getting it. "You're his dad."

"And that won't change. But you need to have the title of mother. You are his mother."

She pinched the bridge of her nose and fought the sting in her eyes. "I don't know what to say."

"Say you will allow me to do this."

He was giving her Oliver. In a way that made him legally hers. *Theirs*. They would share Oliver. He wasn't proposing love or marriage. Silly her, his words had tripped her up. He was proposing a partnership.

"I thought you would want this," he said softly. His gaze, dark and melting, connected with hers. "This is something I can give you. You will legally be his mother. You will call the shots. If there comes a time when you think I'm not the best thing for him…"

"You're such a silly man." She leaned in and kissed his cheek, fighting the urge to tell him what she really thought, and felt. "Thank you for doing what you think is right. But I don't think a day will come when you aren't fit to be his father. You just proved that you're a dad, that you care about him, that you're willing to sacrifice to make him happy. I hate leaving, because he will miss you." She drew in a breath and allowed herself to admit the truth. "I'll miss you."

She got up and walked inside.

Maria was waiting for her inside. Oliver was sleeping and Marcus's little sister had obviously guessed what her brother had been up to.

"Is he playing the martyr?" Maria asked. "He always has, you know. He pretends he doesn't care. I think he cares too much."

"That might be it. And he doesn't trust himself," Lissa told the younger woman. "I don't know how to convince him…"

She stopped herself from saying the words.

If she couldn't say them to herself, she wouldn't say them to someone else.

Maria's expression turned all ornery little sister. "Maybe you should tell him."

"I don't think so." Because she'd overheard his opinion of her. He might think she was a great mom for his son, but to him she was a thorn in his side.

She brushed hair back from Oliver's face and he blinked, waking up to smile at her. "Hey, almost time for lunch."

"Is it chicken?" he asked.

"I think it is." She smiled at the question because he asked it several times a day. He loved chicken.

He sat up, yawned and stretched. And then he looked at her, reaching to trace a finger down her cheek. His eyes narrowed and he looked at the other cheek.

"Why are you crying?"

"Because we leave today. Remember? And I think we will both be sad when we leave."

Oliver nodded and then he hugged her. "But we can always come back. Aunt Essie said so."

"Right, we can always come back." She reached for his hand. When she turned around, Marcus was there. He didn't look as if he would cry, but he also didn't look like a man ready to say goodbye.

Chapter Fifteen

The dozer moved over the cleared land. All traces of the home he'd bought were gone. Nothing but bare dirt. Marcus couldn't help thinking of those days as a kid when he'd high-tailed it to this house, to the front porch with its old rocking chairs.

The memories had kept him solid through a lifetime of ups and downs. The memories weren't gone. It had taken him a while to realize that he still had pieces of the Brown family. They were *his* memories, the life lessons they'd taught him. The faith they'd encouraged him to find. He could train just about any horse he got hold of—because of the Browns.

One of those horses happened to be under him at the moment. A solid red chestnut. She had a splash of white on her nose. That was it.

She would make a good little horse for Oliver. That was why he'd bought her.

He hadn't seen his son in three weeks. Not since a pretty June day when Lissa had brought him down to go fishing. She'd kept her distance, acting as if they didn't even know each other. It had unsettled him. And then she'd told him they were going on vacation with her foster parents. She hoped he wouldn't mind. A week in Florida and then she'd be back to work. So it might be a while before he saw Oliver again. She had smiled and told him she would leave him the whole month of July, if Marcus wanted.

It had felt all wrong, that visit had. Oliver hadn't talked much. Lissa had been distant. Marcus had felt as if he had royally messed up. He had felt that way a time or two in his life. When he overrode a bull and got tossed. When he had pushed too hard against his dad.

But this time it cut him to the core unlike ever before.

Alex pulled up, getting out of his truck with that silly grin he wore most of the time these days, now that everyone knew Marissa and Alex would have a baby in the fall. And Lucy, a month or two later.

Maria was planning her wedding to the pretty boy from Fort Worth.

Essie seemed to be dating Marissa's grandpa Dan.

The whole world was going crazy.

"What has you looking like you ate lemons for breakfast?" Alex asked as he approached the arena.

"Nothing. What do you think of Pepper?"

"You named the horse Pepper?" Alex teased.

"Red Pepper."

Eyebrows shot up. "Gotcha. She's pretty small for a big boy like you. You might try riding a grown-up horse."

"Go. Away." He turned Pepper in a tight circle and then took her around the arena again.

"You've convinced me. You've definitely moved up to pony class," Alex called out. "So, are you going to build a house or just sleep in our spare bedroom for the rest of your life?"

"I guess if you want me out, I can move in with Essie."

Alex put a booted foot on the rail of the arena. "I don't think Essie wants you, either. And before you ask, Lucy doesn't have room."

"Why don't you all just take me down a dirt road and leave me. Maybe someone will take me in."

"I doubt it. You're mangy and bad-tempered. Rebuild your house, Marcus. You need a place for your son to visit. And maybe someday, when you're thinking straight, you'll start dating. I hear Oliver's mom is a decent catch."

"Go away. I'm giving you thirty seconds to get back in your truck and go."

Alex laughed. "Right. I'm scared." He rested his arms on the top rail of the fence. "You know that twin thing people are always talking about? You know, feeling each other's pain. Knowing when the other one is in trouble."

"It's a load of horse—"

"Horse tack. Yeah. I knew you'd get all angry." Alex pushed his hat back and Marcus, for the first time in a long time, got the feeling he was looking in a mirror. "Marcus, you're unhappy. You're like a horse with a burr under the saddle. You've convinced yourself you can't have what you most want and it's eating at you. It all comes down to trust. Trust God. Trust yourself. Trust a woman to know her own mind."

"Your thirty seconds are up."

At that, Alex settled his hat back on his hat and headed for his truck. "See you at dinner. Tell Oliver and Lissa hello for me."

Oliver and Lissa? Marcus shook his head and guided the horse on another circuit around the arena. The little mare had an easy gait. She knew her leads. She didn't fuss. He knew she'd make a good first horse.

And then she took him by surprise, rearing up a little and then bucking like a maniac. Burr under the saddle. No. Alex wouldn't do that to him. He held on, wrapping his legs around her middle and holding back on the reins so she couldn't get her head down to pitch him.

When she finally settled, she was shaking. He slid from the saddle and gave her a careful look. She gave herself a good shake and then her head went down as if asking for forgiveness.

"Hey, cowboy, that was quite a ride."

He paused and then faced the woman and little boy standing outside his arena. This time, unlike that time almost two months ago, they were both smiling at him. And he knew two things. One, that the little boy with dark hair was his son. Two, the woman with the brilliant blue eyes had upset his apple cart. He actually knew three things. He had missed them the way he would miss a breath if it was taken from him.

He led the horse to the fence.

"You didn't get thrown." Oliver made the statement sound as if it was the biggest surprise of his life.

"No, I didn't. I didn't expect the two of you."

"We surprised you." Oliver grinned as he said it.

"You sure did. Hey, do you want to brush Pepper? She's pretty good. Usually. And she's yours."

"My own horse?" Oliver didn't wait. He climbed over the fence and landed with a thump next to Marcus. "Can I lead her?"

"You can." Marcus handed the reins to his son, but he stayed close beside them. "Lissa can come, too."

"I don't climb fences," she called out to them.

As they approached the side door to the barn, Oliver looked up. "I call her mom now. Is that okay?"

"What else would you call her?" Marcus took the reins from his son, scooped the boy up and put him in the saddle. "What do you think of that?"

"I like her a lot. And I'm glad I can call her mom." Oliver was quiet for a minute. "I have a mom and I have a dad. You just don't live in the same place. But you both love me."

It sounded like something he'd seen on a children's television program. Marcus wasn't sure he liked that any more than he liked not seeing them more than once a month. But he had made the right decision. He knew that.

He'd given Oliver a mother. He'd given Lissa her son.

He'd given them open doors and opportunity.

He tied Pepper and helped Oliver down. Without waiting for instructions, Oliver found the brush and went to work.

"I think my mom wants to talk to you," Oliver said over his shoulder as he stroked the brush down the mare's neck.

Ginger lipped at Oliver's sleeve, but she minded her manners the way Marcus had known she would.

"Does she really?"

Oliver nodded. "I think you're in trouble. I heard her talking to Grandma Jane about your thick head. I didn't think your head looked thick. But if it is, maybe Doc Parker can help. I think my mom is going to work for him."

Maybe there was something to having a boy who made eavesdropping a serious skill. "Is she really?"

Oliver nodded, but he kept brushing. Marcus stood there for a minute watching his son. After he'd assured himself that Oliver was fine, and with a few final instructions, he headed for the door. Lissa stood there watching them, her hand on Lucky's big head as the dog panted and pushed against her. Buddy, the Labrador they'd rescued after the flood, was still at Alex's. Lucky didn't appreciate being moved and preferred his home with his barn.

"I guess you've taken up eavesdropping, too?" Marcus asked her as he closed the distance between them.

"When necessary. But he didn't tell you anything I didn't know, since it is my plan." Lissa reached for his hand. "What he doesn't know is that I came here to talk to you."

"Did you now?"

He leaned a bit closer, inhaling, because she smelled good. She smelled like sunshine and wildflowers. No wonder Lucky had glued himself to her side and wouldn't budge.

"Don't." She pushed him back.

"Don't what?"

"Don't sniff at me like that hound dog. It's weird. And I need space. Because when I'm done talking, you will either tell me to stay or tell me to go."

"I see." He lost the walking-on-sunshine feeling of a few moments ago. With Lissa looking all serious and giving him ultimatums, maybe he'd just turn tail and head back to the barn and Oliver.

"No, you don't see."

"Okay, I don't see." He studied her face. Brilliant blue eyes, pretty mouth in a firm line.

He knew when to tread lightly. "This is one of those conversations where no matter what I say, I'm in trouble. Right?"

"Not exactly. If you choose wisely, you won't be in trouble."

"Are you taking a job with Doc Parker?"

She poked his shoulder. "Getting ahead of the program, Palermo."

"Hmm, okay."

"I came here to tell you some very hard truths about yourself."

He laughed at that. "And you think you're the first one to ever do that. Lissa, women have been telling me those same things for years. It won't faze me."

"You're wrong." She shook her head. "No, they're wrong. And these are not those same truths."

He started to open his mouth to argue, but something about that spark in her eyes warned him to keep quiet. Rather than talking, he put his hands up in surrender.

"First of all, you are trustworthy. Everyone who knows you has a story to tell about you and how you were there for them or helped them out in a time of need. There are people all over Bluebonnet Springs, and I'm guessing all over Texas, who will rat you out. Second, you need to learn to trust yourself. So what if you were tempted to drink. You didn't. That matters. You are a man your son can count on. You're the man he can model his life after. You're a man of faith and a man of integrity."

"Why do you think I need to hear this?" He was truly curious. And he wanted to keep her there next to him for a little longer.

"Because you doubt yourself. You did everything you could to push us out of your life because you think you are not the man we need. You believe you're not the father your son needs."

He quirked a brow. "Can we go back to the 'we' part?"

"Marcus, you told Pastor Matthews no way would you marry me, that I'm a thorn in your side."

"I didn't realize I had asked you to marry me." Now he was confused. "Or that you'd asked me."

"You're impossible. And I'm not going anywhere, you impossible man. I'm staying here. I'm going to work for Doc Parker because your son has been sad every single day that he hasn't been here. He misses you. He misses your family. He misses his dogs and that pregnant cat."

"She has kittens now."

"Stop trying to distract me."

He held his hands up again. "No way would I do that. So you're staying in Bluebonnet Springs."

"Yes, because your son needs to be here, near you. He needs to see you every day."

He nodded and he very nearly went down on one knee. He was trying to decide his next move when she reached for his hand. She didn't look at him; instead, she focused on interlocking their fingers together. Hopeful. He was starting to feel it again. It was a lightness in his soul.

Who knew?

"I'm not leaving," she said again.

This time he did go down on one knee.

Lissa looked at the man kneeling in front of her. She didn't know what to say or what to do.

"Get up." She pulled on the hand that she still held. She tried to pull free. He wouldn't budge.

He grinned up at her, his dark eyes shining, his smile lopsided and sweet.

"What are you doing?" she whispered.

"Finding out just how serious you are about staying in Bluebonnet Springs."

"I'm very serious."

"I'm glad to hear that, because I've decided

not to let you go. I'm scarred up, a recovering alcoholic, sometimes angry, always unpredictable—"

"Obviously," she interrupted.

He put a finger to his lip. "Shh, my turn. I want to be the man that you can trust. I want to be the father my son can look up to. Lissa, you are more than a thorn in my side. You're the woman I want by my side. Forever." He cleared his throat and his words came out raspier than normal. "When I saw you standing there at the fence, everything felt right for the first time in weeks. You were here. And I think you're supposed to be here. I think if there is something we can trust, it is God, and we can trust that He didn't make a mistake when He sent you on this journey to find me."

"Stand up," she whispered, this time because she couldn't stop the flow of tears. "Please stand up."

He came to his feet and he moved close. Slowly, ever so slowly, he leaned down and his lips touched hers. She clung to his shoulders, thankful for his strength, thankful for his presence. Thankful that she had taken a chance and trusted.

He continued to kiss her, backing her against the side of the barn and holding her close as if he treasured her. That was what he made her feel—treasured. He had no idea that he was the man who could be that person for a woman. But she'd unearthed the truth about Marcus Palermo. She had found her way to his heart and he'd stolen hers.

"I love you, Lissa Hart. You are my heart. I'm never going to let you go. And I'm going to build you a house on this land. We're going to fill it with kids and we're going to make memories. We're going to teach our children to laugh, to love and to have faith."

"That's a lot of planning you're doing, Marcus."

"Too soon?"

"I'm the one calling the shots here, remember?" she whispered against his shoulder. "I came here to tell you how the cow ate the cabbage."

"Did you really?"

"Yes, and you took over. The way you always take over."

He kissed her again and then he moved away from her. "Okay, what else did you want to say?"

She pointed and his eyes widened when he saw that they had an audience. The eavesdropper in chief stood in the doorway of the barn.

"Oliver?" Marcus smiled at his son.

"Knock knock."

Marcus groaned. "I hope this is a good one."

Oliver nodded. "It is."

"Okay," Marcus said. "Who's there?"

"Mary."

Marcus laughed and Oliver grinned. Lissa watched, loving them both so much she couldn't stand it. She had missed Marcus. She'd missed his quietness. She'd missed his dry sense of humor. She'd missed him.

"Mary who?" Marcus asked, his gaze sliding her way, and she just smiled because they both knew how this one would go.

"Mary my mom and then we'll be a family." Oliver laughed and jumped, forcing Marcus to catch him or be knocked down. He caught his son and held him tight. With his free arm he pulled Lissa close and she tumbled against him.

"Oliver, I think the answer is yes," Marcus answered as he held them both close. For the first time in weeks, everything felt right. It felt as if Lissa and Oliver were exactly where they belonged.

Oliver leaned in close. "She told Grandma Jane she loves you."

Marcus whispered to his son. "I love her, too. And I'm glad the two of you decided to come back here and force me to admit it."

"Sometimes it's hard to admit the truth," Oliver said in a singsong voice.

"You're right, sometimes we just need help." Marcus spoke in his soft, gruff voice as he took Lissa by the hand.

The three of them walked back up the hill. And she thought they did look very much like a family. A father, a son and a woman who loved them both to distraction.

Epilogue

On a warm day in March, Lissa stood on the hill looking down at the house Marcus had built for them. It was a replica of the old farmhouse but larger and with the wraparound porch she'd suggested. It was also a little farther from the creek than the original. Today it would become her home. And eventually there might be more children, because Oliver said he needed a brother and a sister. He actually thought a couple of brothers and one sister, because girls can be trouble.

"Are you ready?" Marissa asked as she placed the veil on Lissa's head.

She and Marcus had decided to get married there, on the ranch, because it felt right. They were starting their lives where so many memories had been made. They'd built a steeple-shaped arch by the creek and wildflowers grew profusely in the field. It was the most perfect spot they could think of to become husband and wife.

Maria kissed her cheek. "You're a beautiful bride."

Lissa took the spray of bluebonnet flowers from her soon-to-be sister-in-law. In six months they would celebrate Maria's wedding. She wanted a fall wedding. And by then, Marissa and Alex's little girl, Bella, would be walking and she'd be able to toss flowers down the aisle. Today the little girl was content on her great-aunt Essie's lap, with her great-grandfather Dan sitting next to them, giving her his finger to grab hold of.

Lucy led Issy, who would be their flower girl. Jewel would help. Which meant she would throw flowers at the people gathered to celebrate. She seemed to love throwing flower petals. Lissa didn't mind at all. She had told Lucy to relax and let the girls do what they wanted.

Today was her wedding. She didn't care if the flowers got tossed or if the music went flat. She didn't care if the cake fell. Of course, like every bride she wanted a beautiful wedding. She was even happy to see her birth mother, although her foster father would walk her down the aisle and her foster mom had helped pick her dress. They had been the constants in her life. They'd been the first to teach her about unconditional love.

Through their love for each other, Tom and Jane Simms had taught her the truth about marriage. They'd taught her that real love wasn't perfect—it took work, sacrifice and communication. Real love included understanding and forgiveness. Tom and Jane were celebrating their fortieth anniversary. They knew a little bit about love and making marriage work.

If the wedding ceremony itself wasn't perfect, it wouldn't matter. What truly counted was that she had the people around her who mattered most. She knew that God had blessed her beyond measure.

And as the song "Never Alone" began to play, she knew she would never be alone.

She smiled at Tom, her stepfather, and together they stood and watched the flower girls, bridesmaids and groomsmen, including Oliver, make their way down the small rise to the creek. She dabbed at her eyes and drew in a breath. Tom patted her hand on his arm.

"This is good," he told her. "You're going to be fine. Remember, God is in it. Keep Him at the center of this marriage and you'll be fine."

She nodded. "Yes, we will be."

"Time to become Mrs. Marcus Palermo." He sounded choked up and she noticed tears in his eyes. She leaned against his arm and whispered her thanks to him for being her father.

He led her down the path to Marcus, told Marcus to take care of their girl, and then he took his seat next to Jane. They both nodded and smiled, giving her their blessing.

But it was the man next to her who mattered most. He was her future. He was her other half.

"I love you," he whispered.

"I love you back."

Pastor Matthews cleared his throat. "My turn to talk."

He started the ceremony and the rest was a blur. The only thing that mattered was that God had brought them together. God had made them a family.

And the rest of their lives was ahead of them.

* * * * *

If you loved this story,
pick up the other books in the miniseries
BLUEBONNET SPRINGS

SECOND CHANCE RANCHER
THE RANCHER'S CHRISTMAS BRIDE

from bestselling author Brenda Minton

And be sure to check out
these other great books

HER RANCHER BODYGUARD
THE RANCHER'S FIRST LOVE
THE RANCHER'S SECOND CHANCE
THE RANCHER TAKES A BRIDE
A RANCHER FOR CHRISTMAS

Available now from Love Inspired!

Find more great reads at
www.LoveInspired.com

Dear Reader,

I'm so glad we were able to spend time together in Bluebonnet Springs, Texas. I hope you enjoyed the Palermo family, Essie's café and the other characters in this series. I think it's rather fitting to end the series with the story of Marcus Palermo. He seemed to need a happy-ever-after. Thanks to the arrival of Lissa Hart and a little boy named Oliver, Marcus will find a path to love and happiness.

I think the Palermo family are an example of the healing that comes from finding faith and in not giving up. They were abused, broken and lost, but each of them found a way to take back what was taken and make new lives from the old.

I hope you enjoyed their stories and I hope you'll stick around for my next miniseries. I've caught myself singing the song "Oklahoma" around the house recently. Hint hint…

Blessings,
Brenda

Get 4 FREE REWARDS!

We'll send you 2 FREE Books
plus 2 FREE Mystery Gifts.

Love Inspired® Suspense books feature Christian characters facing challenges to their faith... and lives.

FREE Value Over **$20**

YES! Please send me 2 FREE Love Inspired® Suspense novels and my 2 FREE mystery gifts (gifts are worth about $10 retail). After receiving them, if I don't wish to receive any more books, I can return the shipping statement marked "cancel." If I don't cancel, I will receive 4 brand-new novels every month and be billed just $5.24 each for the regular-print edition or $5.74 each for the larger-print edition in the U.S., or $5.74 each for the regular-print edition or $6.24 each for the larger-print edition in Canada. That's a savings of at least 13% off the cover price. It's quite a bargain! Shipping and handling is just 50¢ per book in the U.S. and 75¢ per book in Canada*. I understand that accepting the 2 free books and gifts places me under no obligation to buy anything. I can always return a shipment and cancel at any time. The free books and gifts are mine to keep no matter what I decide.

Choose one: ☐ **Love Inspired® Suspense**
Regular-Print
(153/353 IDN GMY5)

☐ **Love Inspired® Suspense**
Larger-Print
(107/307 IDN GMY5)

Name (please print)

Address   Apt. #

City   State/Province   Zip/Postal Code

Mail to the **Reader Service:**
IN U.S.A.: P.O. Box 1341, Buffalo, NY 14240-8531
IN CANADA: P.O. Box 603, Fort Erie, Ontario L2A 5X3

Want to try two free books from another series? Call 1-800-873-8635 or visit www.ReaderService.com.

*Terms and prices subject to change without notice. Prices do not include applicable taxes. Sales tax applicable in N.Y. Canadian residents will be charged applicable taxes. Offer not valid in Quebec. This offer is limited to one order per household. Books received may not be as shown. Not valid for current subscribers to Love Inspired Suspense books. All orders subject to approval. Credit or debit balances in a customer's account(s) may be offset by any other outstanding balance owed by or to the customer. Please allow 4 to 6 weeks for delivery. Offer available while quantities last.

Your Privacy—The Reader Service is committed to protecting your privacy. Our Privacy Policy is available online at www.ReaderService.com or upon request from the Reader Service. We make a portion of our mailing list available to reputable third parties that offer products we believe may interest you. If you prefer that we not exchange your name with third parties, or if you wish to clarify or modify your communication preferences, please visit us at www.ReaderService.com/consumerschoice or write to us at Reader Service Preference Service, P.O. Box 9062, Buffalo, NY 14240-9062. Include your complete name and address.

LIS18

Get 4 FREE REWARDS!

We'll send you 2 FREE Books plus 2 FREE Mystery Gifts.

Harlequin® Heartwarming™ Larger-Print books feature traditional values of home, family, community and most of all—love.

FREE Value Over $20

YES! Please send me 2 FREE Harlequin® Heartwarming™ Larger-Print novels and my 2 FREE mystery gifts (gifts worth about $10 retail). After receiving them, if I don't wish to receive any more books, I can return the shipping statement marked "cancel." If I don't cancel, I will receive 4 brand-new larger-print novels every month and be billed just $5.49 per book in the U.S. or $6.24 per book in Canada. That's a savings of at least 19% off the cover price. It's quite a bargain! Shipping and handling is just 50¢ per book in the U.S. and 75¢ per book in Canada*. I understand that accepting the 2 free books and gifts places me under no obligation to buy anything. I can always return a shipment and cancel at any time. The free books and gifts are mine to keep no matter what I decide.

161/361 IDN GMY3

Name (please print)

Address   Apt. #

City   State/Province   Zip/Postal Code

Mail to the Reader Service:
IN U.S.A.: P.O. Box 1341, Buffalo, NY 14240-8531
IN CANADA: P.O. Box 603, Fort Erie, Ontario L2A 5X3

Want to try two free books from another series? Call 1-800-873-8635 or visit www.ReaderService.com.

*Terms and prices subject to change without notice. Prices do not include applicable taxes. Sales tax applicable in N.Y. Canadian residents will be charged applicable taxes. Offer not valid in Quebec. This offer is limited to one order per household. Books received may not be as shown. Not valid for current subscribers to Harlequin Heartwarming Larger-Print books. All orders subject to approval. Credit or debit balances in a customer's account(s) may be offset by any other outstanding balance owed by or to the customer. Please allow 4 to 6 weeks for delivery. Offer available while quantities last.

Your Privacy—The Reader Service is committed to protecting your privacy. Our Privacy Policy is available online at www.ReaderService.com or upon request from the Reader Service. We make a portion of our mailing list available to reputable third parties that offer products we believe may interest you. If you prefer that we not exchange your name with third parties, or if you wish to clarify or modify your communication preferences, please visit us at www.ReaderService.com/consumerschoice or write to us at Reader Service Preference Service, P.O. Box 9062, Buffalo, NY 14240-9062. Include your complete name and address.

HW18

HOME *on the* RANCH

YES! Please send me the **Home on the Ranch Collection** in Larger Print. This collection begins with 3 FREE books and 2 FREE gifts in the first shipment. Along with my 3 free books, I'll also get the next 4 books from the Home on the Ranch Collection, in LARGER PRINT, which I may either return and owe nothing, or keep for the low price of $5.24 U.S./ $5.89 CDN each plus $2.99 for shipping and handling per shipment*. If I decide to continue, about once a month for 8 months I will get 6 or 7 more books, but will only need to pay for 4. That means 2 or 3 books in every shipment will be FREE! If I decide to keep the entire collection, I'll have paid for only 32 books because 19 books are FREE! I understand that accepting the 3 free books and gifts places me under no obligation to buy anything. I can always return a shipment and cancel at any time. My free books and gifts are mine to keep no matter what I decide.

268 HCN 3760 468 HCN 3760

Name   (PLEASE PRINT)

Address   Apt. #

City   State/Prov.   Zip/Postal Code

Signature (if under 18, a parent or guardian must sign)

Mail to the **Reader Service:**

IN U.S.A.: P.O. Box 1867, Buffalo, NY. 14240-1867
IN CANADA: P.O. Box 609, Fort Erie, Ontario L2A 5X3

* Terms and prices subject to change without notice. Prices do not include applicable taxes. Sales tax applicable in NY. Canadian residents will be charged applicable taxes. This offer is limited to one order per household. All orders subject to approval. Credit or debit balances in a customer's account(s) may be offset by any other outstanding balance owed by or to the customer. Please allow 3 to 4 weeks for delivery. Offer available while quantities last. Offer not available to Quebec residents.

Your Privacy—The Reader Service is committed to protecting your privacy. Our Privacy Policy is available online at www.ReaderService.com or upon request from the Reader Service.

We make a portion of our mailing list available to reputable third parties that offer products we believe may interest you. If you prefer that we not exchange your name with third parties, or if you wish to clarify or modify your communication preferences, please visit us at www.ReaderService.com/consumerschoice or write to us at Reader Service Preference Service, P.O. Box 9062, Buffalo, NY. 14240-9062. Include your complete name and address.

READERSERVICE.COM

Manage your account online!

- Review your order history
- Manage your payments
- Update your address

---

*We've designed the
Reader Service website
just for you.*

Enjoy all the features!

- Discover new series available to you, and read excerpts from any series.
- Respond to mailings and special monthly offers.
- Browse the Bonus Bucks catalog and online-only exculsives.
- Share your feedback.

Visit us at:
ReaderService.com

RS16R